DIVIDED

A Seventeen Series Novel

Suzanne Lowe

© SILVERGUM PUBLISHING

The Seventeen Series

Book Three

This edition published 2023
Silvergum Publishing Pty Ltd
www.silvergumpublishing.com

National Library of Australia Cataloguing-in-Publication entry:

Lowe, Suzanne, author.
ISBN: 978-0-6489049-4-6 (print)
ISBN: 978-0-6489049-5-3 (ebook)

For Young Adults.
Subject: Young Adult Fiction, Science Fiction/Australia

Thank you to Steve, Tahlia and Emilie

Family means everything.

CHAPTER ONE

"And he came to us as one unknown, without a name, without a home. To free us from our toils."

Why did the quote she had once studied in English class keep running through Lexi's head?

The sight of the stranger in the distance, shimmery and mysterious in the summer heat, had given her goosebumps. There hadn't been anyone new in town for months, and the last time she had set eyes upon an adult was almost two years ago. Questions and notions swirled around her mind. *Who were they? Where had they come from? Were they alone?*

As she rushed down the sandy bush track with her sister Hadley and friend Braydon by her side, the familiar tug of anxiety knotted in her stomach. Her worn Converse shoes slapped the hot ground, sharp little stones pressing through the thin soles. Lexi took a deep breath, trying to force her shoulders to relax. She slowly released her tightly clenched fists and shook them. "It will be fine," she murmured.

Memories of Broc and his gang invaded Lexi's thoughts making her palms sweat. Ever since Lexi and the other children of Jasper's Bay had their encounter with Broc, she had found it a struggle to control her anxiety. Her heart would pound in her chest, the air catching in her lungs, making breathing difficult. His rough and bullying behaviour towards her and the other children had left an emotional mark on her.

1

SUZANNE LOWE

As she squinted ahead through the afternoon glare, Lexi peered towards the newcomer. She bit the side of her mouth. Thankfully, he had not yet seen nor heard them coming, and she liked that. It gave her time to study him a while longer. She could see he wore black baggy jeans and a long oversized grey hoody with the hood pulled over his head. He stood confidently with his hands on his hips and feet splayed apart.

He must be boiling wearing a sweater in this heat!

Lexi looked down at her own bare, pink-tinged arms covered in fine perspiration. She raised her eyebrows; it must have been at least 35 degrees Celsius today. Too hot for a sweater!

As they ran on towards the farm, the sound of Hadley breathing heavily beside her drew her attention. Lexi glanced sideways at her and saw that even though she was struggling to run with Polo, their dog in her arms, a huge, excited grin covered her face. Lexi's own face remained blank. Her hands formed tight balls as her stomach continued to churn.

Before they reached the stranger, Braydon reached over and gently grabbed Lexi's arm, making her flinch as his fingers brushed her sunburn. She slowed her pace to a fast walk and turned to look at him.

"How shall we approach this?" He asked, drawing deep breaths, and jerking his head towards the newcomer.

Lexi wiped the sweat from her brow. Her face was flushed from the exertion, and she ran her tongue over her dry lips. "Let's just see what he's got to say. I want to know where he's come from and if he's alone."

"Uh-huh. And how come he's survived the virus. It could be helpful for us."

Lexi nodded, giving him a wry smile.

Hadley, who had fallen behind, caught up to them. She placed the wiggling Polo on the ground before shaking her head and rolling her eyes. "Geeze, do you two always have to be so serious! I'm just happy there's finally an adult around. It's okay for you guys living out here in your bush camp."

She gestured with her thumb back towards the makeshift campsite where Lexi and Braydon were now staying. "Back in town, I have to put up with all the younger kids, and don't get me started on the nine-year-old boys!" She puffed out her cheeks. "I don't care where he's come from. I just want to talk to a grown-up for a change!"

Lexi laughed. "Okay, Hadley, fair enough." She picked up her pace. "Come on, then. Let's go and see who this guy is." The other two followed close behind, with Polo running at their heels, happily wagging his tail as he trotted along.

As the group reached the edge of the Bailey farm, Lexi could see that Katie had come out from the farmhouse to talk to the stranger. She held her little sister Sarah squirming on her hip. Katie struggled to hold onto the baby as Sarah's cheeks flamed red as she grizzled and tried to break free. Eventually, Katie gave up the battle and placed Sarah on the ground by her feet. Sarah immediately stopped whining and began shoving fistfuls of dirt into her mouth. Katie looked at her and sighed.

At the sound of the approaching trio's footsteps, the tall stranger quickly turned around to face them. As he moved, the red dust kicked up under his feet, making Sarah sneeze, and she wiped her hand across her nose. Watching the group approach, the stranger slowly raised his hand and pulled the hoody from his head. Surprisingly, long, blond hair tumbled out. Lexi stepped closer and peered at the stranger's face. She blinked twice. It was not a man as she had expected. It was a woman! A very tall woman.

"Hi there," the woman smiled broadly, extending her hand. "My name is Rebekka."

"Oh, hi," replied Lexi looking up at her. "I'm Lexi. And this is Braydon and Hadley." Lexi pointed to the others before taking Rebekka's outstretched hand and tentatively shaking it. It seemed a very formal introduction to Lexi, who glanced at the woman's hand.

Surprisingly, her hand was smooth and manicured, unlike the rough, work-worn hands of the children of Jasper's Bay. A brief frown crossed Lexi's brow as she stared at the woman's hand before dropping it.

"Hey!" squealed Hadley, breaking Lexi's thoughts. She waved enthusiastically as she pushed past Lexi. "It's great to meet you! How did you get here? Are you by yourself? How come you're not sick?" Hadley blurted out questions rapidly like a miniature chihuahua barking excitedly.

Rebekka took a step back and held up her hands. "Whoa."

"Sorry," giggled Hadley, bouncing up and down on her toes. "I'm just excited to see someone new. We've been on our own for quite a while now, and we haven't seen a grown-up for ages!"

Rebekka smiled as she nodded. "Is that so?" she said, looking around. "It seems as though you're doing alright." She gestured to the small herd of black and white cows huddled by the fence and the newly growing field of corn.

Hadley was about to respond when baby Sarah suddenly let out an ear-piercing cry. She arched her back and yelled as Katie struggled to pick her up from the ground. Sarah had rubbed the red dirt in her hair and gotten some in her eye.

"I'd better take her inside," exclaimed Katie as she quickly turned towards the farmhouse, the bellowing, squirming baby now slung over her shoulder. "I'll see you all a bit later."

Hadley raised her hand. "Good luck, Katie."

"You sure you don't need any help?" asked Lexi, watching Sarah writhing around like a fish on a hook, trying to escape. Looking after a toddler when you were only a child yourself was not an easy task!

"No. We're all good. I'll walk into town with her this afternoon," replied Katie as she hooked her toe under the farmhouse screen door and flung it open before quickly manoeuvring inside.

Lexi turned back towards Rebekka. She could see the woman following Katie and Sarah with her eyes, watching them walk up the shaded steps. She had a gleam in her eye. "Well. That looks like a comfortable place," Rebekka smiled, moving to follow Katie inside.

Lexi quickly angled her body to stand in front of Rebekka. "Umm. Actually, I think we should stay out here." Her eyes flicked from the farmhouse and back to Rebekka. She didn't want Rebekka to go inside the house just yet. After all, they still knew nothing about her or if she was alone or part of a bigger group.

Rebekka took another step forward.

"No, really," said Lexi, firmly placing her hand on Rebekka's arm. "I think Katie wants to put Sarah to bed, and we would only disturb her."

Rebekka stared at the farmhouse but did not move any closer. Her lips were pursed together, and Lexi wondered if she should say something further.

Dropping her hand, Lexi opened her mouth to speak when Rebekka abruptly swivelled on her foot and turned her back on her. Rebekka's gaze settled on Hadley.

"So, Hadley, is it?"

Hadley nodded, grinning.

"Tell me how many people are in your group?" Rebekka asked. "Surely not just you five?"

"Well…"

Lexi laughed. "No, not just us five," she said vaguely as she interrupted Hadley, who looked indignant at being unable to answer for herself. "How many did you say were with you?"

Rebekka cleared her throat. "Oh, it's just me," the corner of her mouth turned up a little. "I'm on my own."

"Oh, wow. That must have been hard." Lexi peered around, looking at the hot, barren landscape, but could not see any vehicle, horse or even a bicycle. Without fuel, the town of Jasper's Bay no longer had any working cars, motorbikes, tractors or working vehicles of any kind. The children mostly moved around on foot. Although a few of them had bicycles and skateboards, Lexi could not imagine travelling very far on one of those.

"How on Earth did you get here?" she asked.

Rebekka blinked. "Well, it's a long story." She wiped the perspiration from her forehead with the back of her hand.

Lexi looked at the woman and smiled. "Why don't we all sit in the shade, and you can tell us." She motioned towards a tall, white ghost gum tree with wide branches and dark green leaves. "You must be hot."

"I'll get us some water," suggested Hadley skipping towards a big wooden barrel sitting on the farmhouse porch. She brought back four mismatched plastic mugs of water, trying not to spill them as she walked with two in each hand.

"You have water!?" exclaimed Rebekka as she reached for one of the cups. Her eyes widened. "I didn't think there was *any* water in this damn desert!"

"Yes, we have. But not much. We gather it by hand from Bryer's Creek," explained Braydon, who had been quiet until now. "At least it's fresh." He winked at Hadley as he took a mug from her.

Waiting for Hadley to sit with the group, Rebekka drained her cup, licked her top lip, and began telling her story. "So, I'm from Perth originally. I left when things started to get bad. I couldn't stand the stinking, rotting rubbish and filth everywhere. The smell was awful."

Rebekka looked towards the distant hills. "People had stopped going to work, and anyone who died from the virus or fighting…"

"It's okay," said Lexi. "Go on."

"Well, the dead were simply left in their houses, or worse, in the streets. Rats and other vermin scurried everywhere, and packs of dogs soon started roaming the streets scrounging for food." Rebekka looked at the children listening to her and rubbed her nose as if remembering the smell.

"Yeah," nodded Hadley, wrinkling her nose as well. "We remember. We're from Perth, too. It was horrible!" She shivered and glanced at Lexi, who was staring at Rebekka, her mouth turned down.

"Right. Well, you're a long way from home like me then." Rebekka patted Hadley's hand.

"Where did you go?" Lexi asked, her eyes bright.

Rebekka scratched her head. "Oh well, you know. I went to lots of different towns before I got here. I never saw very many people, though. No adults, mostly kids. They would always run away from me if I tried to talk to them, so I just kept going."

"But where's all your stuff?" asked Hadley, looking at Rebekka's dusty clothing. Polo enthusiastically sniffed her dirty boots, and Rebekka roughly pushed him away.

Rebekka nodded towards a large, oversized Khaki backpack leaning against one of the fences. "I was on a motorbike, so I couldn't carry much besides food, a few personal things and spare fuel." She waved a fly away from her face and peered into her empty cup.

Braydon, who had been listening intently, looked from Rebekka to the backpack. "So, where's your bike? I'd love a go."

Rebekka gave a light tinkling laugh. "Sorry, Kiddo. I had to ditch it a while back when I ran out of fuel. Didn't judge how far it was between towns and ran out of petrol."

"Maybe the fuel had deteriorated and didn't work as well?"

"Yeah, it could be. Anyway, I've been walking ever since, and now, here I am.

The flies buzzed incessantly around the group, and Lexi waved her hand in front of her face trying to deter one from going up her nose. "How did you not get the virus?" she asked, squinting at Rebekka.

"Do you think I could have a little more water? I've walked a long way." Rebekka held out her cup to Lexi, her polished nails glistening in the sun. Lexi stared at the perfect nails.

Rebekka noticed her staring and held out her hand, showing off her nails. "Like them? I do like to keep myself well groomed." She pointedly looked at Lexi's bitten fingernails. "Even in the bush."

Lexi self-consciously curled her fingers and placed her hands in her lap.

Hadley noticed Lexi's red face. "Umm, I'll get it," she offered, jumping to her feet. Taking Rebekka's mug from her hand, she raced towards the house. "Come on, Polo," she called over her shoulder. "Want some water, Boy?" The little dog charged after her, kicking up the red dirt with his paws.

"She's got a lot of energy!" observed Rebekka, laughing.

"Yes, she has," agreed Lexi watching her sister as she skipped back towards them. Lexi pulled her shirt away from her body and flapped the material, trying to generate some cool air. Even in the shade, the heat was making her sweat.

"What is the name of your town, again?" asked Rebekka, gulping the water when Hadley returned.

"It's Jasper's Bay," said Hadley excitedly before flopping to the ground. "And we're very happy to have you." She bowed playfully, leaning forward. "There are only eighteen kids in town, so it's not too crowded. And no adults. Although Lexi thinks she's one," Hadley laughed.

Lexi shook her head slightly.

Hadley ignored her. "Lexi is seventeen, so I suppose she's practically an adult. She and Braydon are the oldest, and they run the town."

"Is that right?" said Rebekka, raising her eyebrows.

"We don't run the town, Hadley. There's a council," said Lexi, winding a piece of her hair around her finger and jiggling her foot.

"Oh, you know you do," Hadley exclaimed, shoving her sister on the arm. "Lexi and Braydon have to stay out here now though because…."

"Hadley!" interrupted Lexi as she quickly stood and grabbed Hadley's arm, pulling her to her feet. "Can I have a word, please?" Her fingers gripped Hadley's sleeve tightly.

Rebekka smiled at them as she watched Lexi pull Hadley away. "What was *that* all about?"

Braydon took a drink from the flask at his hip and stared after the girls. He gave a slight cough. "Oh, you know. Just being sisters." Grabbing a stick from the ground, he started drawing patterns in the dirt.

Rebekka looked at him a little while longer before turning her attention back to the two sisters.

Lexi's face was flushed as she glared at Hadley. "What do you think you're doing, Hadley?"

"I'm not doing anything."

"Yes, you are. You're telling Rebekka everything about the town. About *me*." Lexi pointed at her chest. "We don't know her, and anyway, it's private!"

Hadley pulled her arm free from Lexi's grasp, puffed out her cheeks and sighed. "Okay. Okay, I won't tell her about you and the virus," she whispered, pointing towards the flask of fresh remedy attached to Lexi's belt. "But I think you're being too paranoid. She's an adult. She can help us." Hadley looked back towards Rebekka and waved.

Lexi groaned. "Don't do that. She'll know we are talking about her."

"Well, obviously, we are talking about her. We moved away from her, didn't we? I'm just being friendly." She reached for the flask on Lexi's hip. "You should take some."

"I don't need it."

"Yes, you do; your face is red. The virus is making you jumpy."

Lexi looked down at her hands. They were shaking a little. Maybe Hadley was right. Was the virus making her jittery? She unclipped the flask and took a long drink of the fruity liquid. Closing her eyes for a moment, she took a deep breath. She could feel Rebekka's eyes on her back.

"Just don't tell her anymore about Braydon and me, alright? She doesn't need to know we have the virus or the remedy." She looked into Hadley's eyes. "At least not until we know more about her."

Hadley patted Lexi's arm. "Alright. No more talk about you and Braydon. But I can talk about me, right?" she grinned.

"Sure, Hadley. Tell her all about you." Lexi shook her head and laughed. "I'm sure she will love that."

"What's not to love!" Hadley laughed too as she skipped back to Rebekka and Braydon.

"Come on, Rebekka," Hadley grinned, reaching for Rebekka's hand. "Let's leave this boring farm. Let me show you, our town."

Watching her sister go, Lexi gathered the scattered mugs and returned them to the porch. Cupping her hands around her eyes, she peered through the front windows of the farmhouse and could see Katie and Sarah fast asleep on their living room couch.

The little girl had her thumb tightly jammed into her mouth, and Katie's arm was splayed wide as Sarah lay stretched out on her chest. Smiling, Lexi quietly walked down the steps and made her way back to Braydon, who was waiting for her under the tree.

The pair lingered for a moment, letting Rebekka and Hadley walk a little way ahead before following behind. Lexi wanted a chance to gather her thoughts. She rubbed her hands up and down on her pants as she watched Rebekka walking beside Hadley.

Her green backpack was slung over her shoulder, and her head was bent slightly towards Hadley as if listening to what she had to say. Lexi hoped Hadley kept her word about not talking about her and the virus.

Looking down, she took Braydon's hand in her own. It was hot like hers, but she didn't mind. "I suppose it will be good to have an adult in town again. She seems nice." Lexi glanced sideways at him.

"Yeah, she *seems* nice."

Stopping, Lexi turned to face Braydon. "You don't think so?"

He tucked one of his curls behind his ear. Lexi loved those curls. They were just like little springs all over his head. "I don't know. It's so hard to tell. I thought Katie and Lilly's brother, Kevin was alright, and look how he turned out!"

Lexi remembered back to a few months ago when Kevin had joined a gang of kids from out of town. One night, they started a fight, and things soon became heated and out of control. Kevin's sister Lilly had died that night at the hands of her own brother, and Zac was badly injured. The children of Jasper's Bay were all still reeling from the shock. It was as though someone had sliced a part of their innocence away, leaving them raw.

Lexi shook her head to clear her thoughts before stretching her arms around Braydon's waist and resting her head on his chest. "Hadley thought I was being paranoid because of the effects of the virus," she said, biting her thumb nail.

Braydon shrugged. "Hmm, I guess she could be right." He examined Lexi's face as she chewed on her lip. "Let's just wait and see. I know Hadley wouldn't think so, but it's good to be cautious. Maybe she's found out some more information from Rebekka. I'd still like to know how an adult has survived the virus this long." Lexi nodded in agreement.

Not wanting the others to get too far ahead, they returned to the road and continued walking along the dusty red track. Without the constant traffic of cars and other vehicles travelling along the path, yellow and green weeds had sprung up along the road. Cracks had begun to form in the dry earth, making it look like a patchwork quilt.

"Well, if anyone can get someone to talk, it's Hadley."

"That's if they get the *chance* to talk!"

Lexi laughed and nodded. "Yes. That's if they get the *chance* to talk." She started to trot, pulling Braydon along behind her. "Come on, let's catch up to them. I want to hear what else our newcomer has to say. You know, it might be nice not to be the oldest in town for once."

11

CHAPTER TWO

The inside of the little church of Jasper's Bay was stifling hot. The air was thick and suffocating though most of the children did not seem to care as they stared intently at the strange new woman standing on the stage in front of them. Beside her stood the town's small council of Lexi, Braydon, Jason, Logan, and Zac.

As Lexi stepped forward to introduce Rebekka, the noise in the small, confined room rose to a loud ruckus. Children excitedly called out questions as most of them stood and moved forward in a rush. Lexi tried to raise her voice above the clammer to quieten them as she could see several younger children with their hands over their ears, their eyes darting around the room. One little boy had started to cry as he huddled in his seat while the older children around him called out loudly.

"Please sit back down. We can't hear you if you are all calling out!"

The children ignored her.

A trickle of sweat ran down the back of Lexi's spine as her nervousness at speaking in front of crowds closed in on her. She cleared her throat several times and tried again.

"Everyone! We need you to...."

"Ahem!" Rebekka abruptly stepped towards the front. She pushed past Lexi and raised her arm in the air with her fingers pointed to the ceiling.

A hush quickly fell over the room as the children immediately sat and became silent. They stared up at Rebekka as though she were a schoolteacher, and they were in her class.

Lexi turned to Braydon; her eyebrows raised. Braydon shrugged, smiling.

Maybe having an adult around would be a good thing!

Rebekka scanned the room as she waited for the children to settle.

"I know you probably have many questions to ask me," she said, slowly lowering her arm to her side. "So let me first say I have come here to help you." Her eyes darted towards Lexi for a moment before returning to the crowd.

Lexi opened her mouth before closing it and biting her lip.

"I've travelled all the way from Perth to be with you," Rebekka explained. "You see, I've lost all my family and friends, so I need a new place to stay." She held her arms in front of her with her hands face up before opening them widely.

"You can stay at my house!" called out a little girl with messy blonde hair sitting in the front row. She grinned up at Rebekka, her two front teeth missing.

"Well, thank you, little miss," smiled Rebekka winking at her. "Perth was not very nice in the end. Too many mangy dogs and mongrels. Your town is much nicer."

The little girl nodded, looking up at Rebekka, captivated.

"How come you didn't die?" asked a boy, raising his hand. "My Mum and Dad died."

"Yeah, do you have to take the bush remedy, too?" asked another.

Rebekka's eyes lit up, and she cocked her head to the side, peering out into the crowd. "What's the bush remedy?"

Lexi quickly stepped beside Rebekka, laughing nervously. "Um, Rebekka, thank you for answering some of our questions." Lexi rubbed at her eyebrow. "Would you mind stepping outside the church for a moment?"

Rebekka swivelled her head and looked at her sharply. Lexi's cheeks turned pink.

"It's just that we need to have a quick talk as a group. We won't be long. Hadley, can you show Rebekka outside." She gestured to Hadley, who scampered over to join them.

Rebekka hesitated for a moment before following Hadley outside the church. Lexi noticed her hand rapidly tapping her thigh. She obviously wasn't happy at being asked to leave.

As Lexi peered out at the crowd of children, her right eye twitched. With Rebekka gone, they had already started talking loudly again. Jostling each other as they bounced up and down in their seats. She raised her arm the same way Rebekka had done, but the others just ignored her, continuing to talk over the top of each other. She rolled her eyes and groaned before reaching for a large wooden ruler resting on the podium.

Banging the ruler several times, Lexi waited until the children turned to face her. It took a while for them to settle, as naturally, they all wanted to talk about Rebekka. Once Lexi had their attention, she stepped to the front and gestured for the other council members to join her.

"I know this is all very exciting, but we must remember that we don't actually know anything about Rebekka. Just because she's an adult doesn't mean we should immediately trust her."

A boy with a ripped orange t-shirt stood and booed.

"Hey!" Braydon pointed at him with an outstretched finger. "Sit down and listen."

The boy glared at Braydon before flumping back in his seat.

"We have to decide whether we should let her stay. Do we need an adult? We've been doing alright on our own." She glanced sideways at Jason and gave a slight shrug.

"We can't just let her walk out in the bush. You heard her; she doesn't have anywhere to stay. She might die out there," said Jason in reply.

"We could give her a horse," said someone from the crowd.

Lexi shook her head. "No, we can't. We need the horses for ploughing the fields at the farm." She scratched her head. "I guess she might be able to help us. It could be a trial run." She shrugged and looked out at the crowd before her.

"Yes!" shouted most of the children, clapping their hands and cheering. "Let her stay!"

Lexi turned back to the council, blowing out her cheeks. "Well, I guess it's the right thing to do." She tilted her head. "Let's just see how it goes."

The others nodded.

"She could stay in our old house," suggested Jason looking towards the wooden church doors as Rebekka and Hadley walked back through. "No one is staying there now, and it's a little way out of the main part of town."

"Great idea, mate," agreed Logan patting him on the back.

The group looked towards Rebekka as she made her way back to the tiny stage. The younger children had all rushed to surround her as she walked into the church, and it took her a little while to push past them.

As she climbed the stairs, she looked expectantly at Lexi and the other members of the council.

"You can stay," stated Lexi, picking at a piece of fraying skin around her fingernail. "But we're not looking for a mayor, Rebekka. We have things running nicely here." She looked at Rebekka closely and smiled. "Maybe you can help us improve," she suggested trying to be friendly.

Rebekka smiled back. "Of course. Actually, I am very good at sewing." She glanced around at the children, many of whom had ripped and tattered clothing. "I could help make some new outfits." Her eyes scanned the crowd of children until she found Hadley. "New clothes could be nice," she winked.

Hadley grinned back and clapped her hands, bouncing up and down in her seat.

Lexi glanced at Braydon and shrugged. "Nothing wrong with new clothes."

She watched Rebekka smiling at the younger children and hoped they were making the right decision. If things went wrong, it wouldn't be easy asking her to leave once she had settled in.

Later that afternoon, the town lit a small bonfire to celebrate Rebekka joining Jasper's Bay. Fresh sweetcorn was harvested from the field at Bailey's Farm and placed in the hot coals of the fire, ready to roast. The green husks remained on the corn to protect the sweet kernels inside from the fire's intense heat, as even at the fire's edge, the coals were glowing red.

Jakob, one of the older boys in town, had managed to catch several medium-sized fish from Bryer's creek, and after cleaning and scaling them, they, too, were placed in the hot coals.

A delicious aroma soon filled the air, and all around, empty stomachs gurgled and growled in anticipation. Because of the limited food supply in the town, feeling hungry was now an everyday occurrence. The farm supplied Jasper's Bay with sweetcorn, a few eggs from the chickens, plus apples when they were in season and daily milk from the ten dairy cows, which was a blessing, especially for the younger children. Many town children had also established small vegetable gardens in their backyards from seeds, and the occasional fish or yabbie was caught from the creek. However, for the town's eighteen children, it was never enough. Without running water or electricity, tending to the gardens was very labour-intensive; many of the children were under 10 years old, and no one had solved the major problem of keeping the food they managed to grow or catch fresh in the blazing Australian summer heat. Nothing stayed fresh for very long, and flies and other insects were a constant battle. Coming together tonight to enjoy a meal felt special.

As the children stood around the fire enjoying the crackling, blazing flames, their faces were aglow as they watched the embers float high into the black ink sky. There was a buzz of general excitement as a group of children gathered around Rebekka as she sat by the fire in one of the fold-out camp chairs. No one had seen an adult for over a year, and having a new face around and someone different to talk to was refreshing. Seeing the same faces and discussing the same interests for 12 months was monotonous and boring. Even if you did like the person you were talking to, there was only so often you could discuss which used to be your favourite Avengers movie or who you shipped from a favourite TV show. Especially as all those things had now become part of the past. Memories were starting to fade, as were shopping trips, fast food, and school.

Lexi watched the younger children talking and giggling excitedly as they tried to press in close to Rebekka. Rebekka seemed to be enjoying the company and closeness of the others. Her face lit up as she laughed at something one of the children beside her said, and she patted their head.

Lexi held her hand up to her mouth as she whispered to a smaller group of older kids sitting off to the side.

"I still don't understand why Rebekka doesn't have the virus. Is she immune?" Lexi's eyes flicked to Jason.

He shrugged. "That's what I'd like to know too. But she doesn't seem to want to talk about it." Jason scratched the tip of his nose with his finger. "Notice how she changes the subject whenever anyone asks."

"Do you think we can trust her?" asked Logan squinting at Rebekka, who was leaning in close to Hadley as she knelt beside her. "The others all love her."

"It's just because she is new in town. It's like having a new toy to play with." Lexi tilted her head to the side and twisted her hair around her finger as she studied Rebekka. "Plus, she does seem nice."

"Yeah, she does," Braydon took Lexi's hand in his. "Let's just keep a close eye on her. At least until we get to know her better."

The others nodded.

"If she's up to no good, we will soon know." Jason grinned. "Gossip spreads like a wildfire around here!"

"Hey," whispered Lexi as Logan and Jason stood to join the other children. "You're going to have to do most of the observing, I'm afraid."

The pair turned back to face her; Logan had his arm slung loosely over Jason's shoulder.

"Braydon and I will do what we can, but I don't know how much use we will be stuck out at our bush camp," Lexi remarked as she unscrewed the lid on her flask of bush remedy. "Unless she comes out to the farm, of course." She smiled and took a long drink before offering some to Braydon.

"Will do," replied Jason as a loud crack of burning wood sent a fresh shower of sparks into the air. He glanced over his shoulder at the fire and the kids poking a burning log with large sticks and throwing rocks into the flames. "I think we had better check the corn and do some crowd control before someone falls into that fire."

Jason and Logan moved off towards the others. "You know, twelve months ago, that would have been *me* playing with that fire," he grinned.

"It still would be if no one else was watching you," Lexi teased.

Jason playfully stuck his middle finger in the air making Lexi laugh. "Hang on, I'll come and help."

As Lexi moved to stand, Braydon grabbed her arm and gently pulled her back. "Wait, Lexi." He looked up at her. Her long hair hung loose around her shoulders, and her face had the beginnings of sunburn across her nose and cheeks. "I want to talk to you alone for a moment."

Sitting cross-legged on the ground, Lexi leaned forward and placed her hand on Braydon's knee. "What's up?" her eyes twinkled.

Braydon shifted his position to move closer to Lexi and ran his finger tenderly down her cheek to her jaw.

Lexi smiled. The two of them had become close since moving away from the central part of the town and setting up their own makeshift camp.

"I wanted to ask you how things are going between you and Hadley," he whispered. "You two seem tense."

"Oh." Lexi looked down at the ground before taking her hand from Braydon's knee. She cleared her throat. "Well, yeah, I guess you could say that." Glancing towards Hadley, she watched as Hadley chatted animatedly with Rebekka. "We have never been super close like some sisters are. But we did like doing some things together. You know, dancing to the radio or going to the movies. Now all we do is argue about stupid stuff. I guess it doesn't help that we can't do any of those old things anymore." She shrugged her shoulders. "I do worry that we are drifting apart." She peered at Braydon, who simply nodded.

Lexi gave him a half smile in return. "I know. I sound like I'm part of an old married couple complaining that we never do anything together anymore." She held up her two pointer fingers, making quotation marks in the air. "It's true, though, and she's the only family I have left, so…" Lexi stopped abruptly and flicked her eyes to Braydon's. "Sorry." She said tenderly, grabbing his hand and squeezing gently. "At least my sister is here with me. Do you think about *your* sister often?"

Braydon's shoulders slumped. "Yeah, I do. And I hope I get to see her again one day, but I think it would take a miracle. She's in France, and I'm here." He picked up a stick and drew a line in the sand by his feet. The corners of his mouth drooped down. "It's a long way to swim."

Moving to sit closer to him, Lexi placed her arms around Braydon's shoulders and gave him a tight hug. "I shouldn't complain about Hadley."

Braydon placed his hand on hers. It was rough and calloused from hours of working at the farm. "I asked you about her, remember." He turned his body to face Lexi. "She's always in town or on the farm, and we are stuck out at the bush camp. You don't get to see much of her anymore. You just have to make your times together more meaningful."

Lexi glanced at her sister once again. "She just seems to always to want to argue with me." She waved her hand about her face in irritation at a mosquito that buzzed incessantly around her ear.

Braydon chortled. "That's what you do with older siblings. I did it to my sister too. I think Hadley is just trying to find her own way and make her own decisions."

"Well, I'm not stopping her," said Lexi frowning. She grabbed Braydon's stick from him and started flicking the small red rocks by her feet.

"You can be a bit bossy with her."

"Bossy!"

Braydon smiled and nodded.

Lexi huffed. "I'm just trying to keep her safe."

"You *are* safe," he stated with his hands out in front of him, palms up. "Stop worrying." He stood and began walking towards the bonfire, his hands shoved in the front pockets of his pants.

Lexi sat a while longer, watching her sister as she discussed something with Rebekka. Hadley had a massive grin on her face, and her cheeks were aglow from the heat of the fire.

"Yeah. I guess we are," Lexi said quietly, biting the inside of her cheek.

At that moment, Rebekka looked away from Hadley and stared directly at Lexi as though she had heard her, with her gaze lingering for just a little too long.

Lexi blinked before quickly looking away. Her eyes darted towards her friends talking to the others beside the campfire. Jason had his arm slung loosely over Logan's shoulders, and they looked happy. Zac, his head bandaged with a thick white cloth, sat with baby Sarah balanced on his knees and his sister Katie by his side. They were reading a story from a little cardboard baby book in the glow of the campfire. Even Braydon, who usually worried as much as she did about things, had returned to the campfire laughing and joking with the others.

Lexi cracked her knuckles. *Why did she feel so unsettled? Was the bush remedy becoming ineffective?*

She looked down at the slight tremor in her fingers before closing her hands into a tight fist. The sound of Braydon and Jason laughing drew her attention back to her friends and she quickly stood, shook her hands, and walked to join them.

With her attention focused on her mates, Lexi had not noticed Rebekka continuing to observe her. Although Rebekka was sitting surrounded by talking children, she was ignoring them. All her attention was on Lexi. Her hands were steepled in front of her chin and a small smile played at the corner of her mouth as she continued to watch.

CHAPTER THREE

The next day was sweltering. There wasn't a single cloud in the blue sky, and the red dirt baked and cracked in the harsh sun. Lexi, Braydon, and Ollie stood in the shade of an old ghost gum tree. Its long white branches and green leaves giving some relief to the children below.

"Where *is* Hadley?" asked Lexi, looking annoyed. She had one hand on her hip and the other up to her face shading her eyes as she peered towards the town.

"We've been waiting here for *ages*. I want to get going before it gets any hotter."

The group had planned an expedition into the bush to look for food and supplies to make the tonic that Lexi and Braydon relied on. A few of the other older children, including Jason, would soon be turning seventeen and in need of the brew as well, so it was essential to keep a ready supply of the bush medicine.

"Look. Here comes Jason and Logan. I wonder what they want?" Braydon raised his hand in the air and waved at the two boys who were heading their way.

Logan waved back. His hair had grown to his shoulders, and he wore it in a loose ponytail to keep it off his neck. Lexi also had her long hair tied back from her face though a few stray strands had escaped, and she tucked them behind her ears as they tickled her cheeks.

"Good morning," greeted Logan cheerfully as he strolled up to the group. "I'm afraid you've got us to help with today's food gathering." He bowed theatrically.

"Where's Hadley?" asked Lexi squinting towards the town. She had been looking forward to spending some time with her sister. They always enjoyed exploring the bushland, looking at the different wildflowers, spotting kangaroos and wallabies and the occasional elusive bilby or quoll.

Jason glanced sideways at Lexi and cleared his throat. "Umm, she asked us to come and help instead."

"What do you mean?"

Jason scratched his chin and shifted his stance. He looked from Logan and back to Lexi. "She's helping Rebekka with some sewing project."

"Sewing project?" Lexi's brow furrowed. "Hadley hates sewing. She couldn't even sew a pillowcase in home economics class at school."

Jason shrugged. "Yeah, I dunno. There's only a few of them doing it."

"So, you've got us instead," laughed Logan grabbing Lexi's hand. "Come on. I thought I'd better learn what bush foods we need to make the remedy anyway." He glanced at Jason and smiled. "I have to look after Jason when he turns seventeen next month and becomes an old man!"

Jason laughed good-naturedly, his eyes twinkling. "Yeah, I know. I'm gonna be an old fart!"

Lexi laughed, "Yeah, you are." She took one more glance over her shoulder towards the town before turning toward the bush.

"Okay, Ollie, lead the way," she said, smiling fondly at the young Aboriginal boy.

Ollie's mum had been a teacher at the local school and had taught him how to gather bush tucker when it was ripe and its many uses. The group had also discovered a book on Aboriginal bush food and medicine in old Mrs Carmody's library. So far, they had successfully found a few bush foods growing in the area, like Billygoat plumbs, Finger limes, Gooseberries, bush tomatoes, and passionfruit.

Plus, Ollie had cleverly concocted a bush remedy from the leaves and flowers of the Sticky Oyster Bush, Native Sage, and Lilly Pilly berries to help the older children with the effects of the KV17 virus. While not a cure, it did help lessen the rages and heat sweats and make life a little more bearable for Lexi and Braydon.

Ollie happily skipped along the little bush track the children had trampled into the dirt on their many forays into the bushland. Lexi held a map in front of her, glancing down at it occasionally. She had drawn a simple diagram of all the locations of bushes and trees where the children had previously found food, and they hiked to each area hoping for some ripe fruit and berries. Many of the fruits had been half eaten by the brightly coloured blue, green and red Lorikeets. However, the children took the damaged fruit anyway, as some remained edible.

"What are these ones called?" Lexi asked Ollie as she plucked a small, round, white, and purple-speckled fruit from a bush with long, thin, green leaves.

"They're Midyim berries," observed Ollie, picking a few himself. "They're really yummy!" He grinned, placing one in his mouth.

Lexi followed his example and popped one into her mouth too. She tentatively bit down on the ripe fruit. A sudden sweet and tangy burst of flavour hit her taste buds like an explosion of sherbet. They tasted a little like blueberries.

"Oh wow," she exclaimed, smiling. "They *are* yummy." She crouched down, helped Ollie pick the remaining berries they could see growing on the small bush, and handed them to the others.

With their woven panadas leaf baskets now half full of fruits, leaves and herbs, the group decided to rest under a cluster of nearby mulga bushes and sample the Midyim berries. The mulgas were in flower, and their long, bright yellow blooms stood out among the harsh Australian bushland.

Lexi knelt on the ground as she added the cluster of Midyim berry bushes to her map using a thin pencil to draw. The hot sun beat down on her back and a layer of perspiration soon covered Lexi's brow. She wiped it away with the back of her hand, leaving a thin smear of dirt. Once she had finished drawing, Lexi again placed one of the juicy fruits into her mouth and bit down on the ripe flesh. She sighed in delight. "Man, they are so good," she exclaimed, her hand on her chest. "Thank you, mother nature. And Ollie."

Ollie beamed in delight.

Jason screwed up his nose. "Not bad, Ollie. But not as good as a chocolate Maccas thick shake," he grinned, offering his second berry to Logan. "You can have mine."

"You and your sweet tooth," laughed Lexi, poking Jason's shoulder with her finger. "A thick shake would be good right now, though," she agreed, licking her lips. "I don't suppose we'll ever have those again." She lay on her back and stared at the cloudless, blue sky. "Or ice cream with Milo sprinkled on top!"

Jason's' eyes glazed over. "Oh yum, Milo. So good!"

"Milo on your ice cream?" questioned Ollie, his head tilted to the side.

Lexi and Jason laughed.

"Oh, mate. It's the best!" Jason grinned. "That malt flavour, yum!"

Ollie looked at Lexi. "I love ice cream," he said wistfully, licking his lips.

"Me too!" Smiled Lexi, putting her arm around his thin shoulders. "Especially chocolate or salted caramel ice cream."

Ollie nodded, grinning.

So many things had changed in the last year, and even though the town of Jasper's Bay and its inhabitants were doing all right, it was hard not to feel annoyed at the childhood they had all lost. Most of their days were now spent looking for, or trying to grow, food. As well as gathering water and firewood and burning waste.

Lexi watched a bee gathering pollen from one of the yellow flowers and sighed. "Guess we're just like you," she murmured as the bee flew to the next flower. An endless quest for water and the next food source.

"What did you say?" asked Braydon, lying on his side next to Lexi.

"Oh, nothing. Just wish I could go back in time for one day."

"What would you do?" he asked, trying to rub the smudge of dirt from her forehead, only making it worse.

"I'd give my parents a big hug and spend the day at the movies with my friends eating salted caramel choc bomb ice creams!" she giggled. "How about you?"

Braydon rolled on his back and closed his eyes, his face relaxed. "I'd spend the day with my sister watching those stupid vampire movies she loves. Then head to the beach to surf until the sun sets," he smiled. "We'd grab fish and chips for dinner and sit on the cool sand watching the sun go down."

Lexi raised herself up onto her arms. "Hot chips! That sounds awesome. I wish we had some potatoes!" she licked her lips at the thought. "I wonder if there are any yabbies left in Bryer's Creek? We haven't caught any for a while."

"Did you say, Yabbies!" exclaimed Jason joining the conversation.

"Yes, I haven't seen any for a few months; I hope we haven't fished them out."

Logan stood and brushed the sand from his pants before offering his hand to Lexi and pulling her up. "Maybe they've just moved further up the river," he shrugged.

Lexi stood beside Logan. "We could spend an afternoon exploring and swimming when we get a free day?"

Logan laughed. "A free day. I think I have less free time now than when I went to school and had homework to do!"

"Yeah, I know. Maybe we should suggest having "duty" free afternoons a couple of times a week. What do you think?"

"Yes, to that," said Jason, brushing the hair from his eyes. "It's always so bloody hot. Even *I* would go for a swim in the creek, and you know how much I hate the outdoors."

Lexi grinned at her friend. "Yes. I was surprised to see you out here today. Bushwalking is not really your thing, is it?" She peered around them. The flat, baked earth was sparsely covered in tall eucalypt trees and the occasional flowering shrub. They had seen black cockatoos, a blue-tongued lizard, and a few kangaroos. Everything else was hiding from the harsh Australian sun.

Jason shrugged. "Ah, well, you know. Anything for my friends," he laughed. "Even at the risk of getting a tan." He pulled up the sleeve of his long shirt to expose his pale skin.

Lexi smiled at him fondly. With his red hair and fair complexion, Jason liked to do his work indoors. She looked at her own hands and forearms. They were covered in scratches and bruises, and the skin was pink from sunburn.

Lexi pulled at Jason's shirt. "Come on," she said. "We had better get back to town before we all start turning red like lobsters," she laughed. "And I want to start brewing a batch of the remedy. Let's get out of this sun." She wiggled her tingling fingers before taking a drink from her hip flask.

"Oh, thank goodness," exclaimed Jason dramatically. "I thought we'd have to stay out here all day!"

He wiped the back of his hand across his brow before picking up his basket of fruit. "Not that this hasn't been fun," he said sarcastically. "But too much vitamin D is definitely not good for my delicate complexion," he stated, rubbing his fingers down his cheeks dramatically and pointing his chin in the air, making everyone laugh. He grinned and winked at Logan, who playfully poked him in the ribs.

As the group of gatherers made their way back into Jasper's Bay, tramping their heavy feet along the dusty red trail, they soon came across a cluster of children on the outskirts of town. The children talked excitedly, waving their arms around animatedly, laughing and whooping.

"Someone's having fun," observed Logan, huffing as he lugged his heavy basket of produce. He stopped and stared at the group. "What *are* they wearing. And why are they all dressed the same?"

All the children in the group wore matching white button-up shirts with a red emblem on the right sleeve. From that distance it was impossible to see the symbol; however, it looked like a simple shape of some sort.

Walking closer, Lexi spotted Hadley with the group. She was sitting with Todd on a large pile of disused limestone blocks. Todd was about Hadley's age, had short black hair and an easy smile. The two had struck up a friendship since the sisters had arrived in Jasper's Bay and were now spending a lot of time together.

Lexi smiled knowingly. "So, that's why she didn't want to come gathering," she said to herself, nodding.

Hadley looked up as she saw the group approaching and waved enthusiastically. She looked as though she were about to burst with excitement. Jumping to her feet, she came skipping towards the group.

"Oh no, here comes trouble," teased Jason as Hadley skidded to a stop in front of them. Poking her tongue at him, Hadley began dancing around on her toes.

"Hey, Hadley, what are you guys up to?" Asked Lexi. Not wanting to start an argument, she didn't mention the fact that Hadley had not come fruit picking as promised.

"And what are you wearing?" exclaimed Logan, pointing at Hadley's white t-shirt.

Hadley spun around on the spot. "Aren't they cool! Bet you wish you had one, Lexi. Rebekka found a box of these shirts in the back of the old JRS clothing store. You know. The one with the broken windows."

"Yes, Hadley. We know the one," chorused the group in unison.

Hadley laughed. "Well, I helped Rebekka sew these red stars on them for us." She pointed happily to the red star on the shoulder of her shirt.

Lexi frowned. "Okay. Why?"

Hadley started bouncing around again. "I don't know. It's for our group. They look cool, don't they?"

Lexi and Braydon exchanged glances.

"What do you mean, *your group.*" Asked Braydon as he lowered his basket of fruit to the ground and placed his hands on his hips.

"I'm not supposed to say," said Hadley, lowering her voice and looking around her.

Lexi leaned in closer to her sister. "Hadley, do you mean *your* group. Or someone else's?"

Hadley rolled her eyes. "Okay, it's Rebekka's group. But I'm in it." She grinned happily, her cheeks turning pink with delight.

Lexi raised her eyebrows. "Rebekka's group! What do you mean Rebekka's group? She's only been in town five minutes!" Lexi leaned forward to examine the star.

"What's up your butt. It's just a bit of fun, Lexi!" Hadley glared with her arms folded tightly across her chest.

Lexi blinked. "Nothing's up my butt." She stood straight and sighed. "I'm just tired. We've been out collecting stuff in the heat all morning." She wiped her hand across her cheek.

Hadley's angry glare quickly faded. "Oh, right. Sorry. I know I was supposed to help." She plucked at her new shirt. Smudges of dirt were already staining the white fabric. "I'll help next time," she promised, taking one of the fruits from Lexi's basket.

"Yummy. These are nice," she exclaimed, biting into the flesh of a bush plumb before turning away from her sister. "Hey, I've got to go, Lexi. Got group stuff to do." She waved her hand as she skipped off.

Before she got too far away, Hadley abruptly stopped, her feet skidding in the dirt, sending a flurry of dust into the air. She quickly turned and came skipping back to the group. Her hand again reached into Lexi's basket and grabbed another of the ripe plumbs. "Better take one for Rebekka. She'll like that."

Hadley grinned from ear to ear. "I'll see you guys later," she called back over her shoulder, her mouth full of plumb.

Lexi's own mouth dropped open as she stared after her sister. "No problem, Hadley. You go and enjoy yourself," she muttered, steam practically coming from her ears.

Braydon looked at Lexi and grabbed her hand. "Come on, Lex," he said quickly. "Let's drop these fruits at the store, then we can go to Logan and Jason's house. I'll help you brew some of the remedy."

"Yes, come on. Let's get out of this heat for a bit," suggested Jason. "I'd offer you a cold drink. But I haven't got one," he laughed, his eyes crinkling at the sides.

Lexi nodded her head but didn't smile. She was staring at the star on Hadley's arm as she ran back towards Todd and the others. Her forehead furrowed, and she rubbed at her right eye. The star reminded her of something. She couldn't remember what, but she didn't think it was anything good.

CHAPTER FOUR

Later that day, Lexi and Braydon walked hand in hand as they left Jason and Logan's home and headed back towards their own. The feeling of his palm touching hers felt comforting, and she squeezed tightly.

As Braydon looked at her, he smiled, his grin a little lopsided. He had been suffering from a toothache the last few days, and Lexi wondered if it still pained him. Ollie had given him some Native Poplar leaves to chew, which helped numb the area, but without a dentist, he just had to endure the ache.

Lexi watched him, feeling the warmness spread throughout her chest. Finding someone she could share the troubles and discomforts of this new world with was a blessing. Being the only two teenagers in the town with the virus wasn't easy. Whilst the others tried to help, none of them understood what Lexi and Braydon were going through. The constant fight and struggle to keep it under control and the rage that simmered just under the surface like a pot of water about to boil over. Sometimes she felt like Eric Banner trying to keep the Hulk at bay, and she was glad that neither she nor Braydon had to face the battle alone. It was bad enough to live away from Hadley and their friends but doing it alone would be a lonely place.

The couple walked along the main street of Jasper's Bay as it stretched all the way from the centre of town to the edge of the Bailey family farm. Braydon and Lexi had walked it many times before, simply placing one foot in front of the other on autopilot as they let their thoughts wander. Today, however, was different.

Just before they reached the outskirts of town, Lexi stopped walking and stood still. Her thoughts had been interrupted by a sound out of place in the bushland. She turned her head back towards the town and listened. *Had she heard some sort of new bird? That didn't seem right. This sound was more mournful.* She listened again and raised her hand for quiet as Braydon opened his mouth to speak.

Then she heard it again. It was someone crying, she was sure of it, and they sounded truly upset. Braydon heard it too. They both swivelled their heads around, trying to locate the source. The voice sounded young and had now become a loud wailing.

"Over there!" suggested Lexi pointing to a small rundown playground. The playground stood next to an old scout hall just before the town's main road ended. She and Braydon hurriedly ran to investigate.

"Is everything alright?" Lexi called out as she looked about. "Do you need help!?" her voice was high with concern.

The wailing intensified.

Lexi looked at Braydon, her eyes wide. *Was one of the younger children injured?*

They hurried closer towards the playground.

Quickly scanning the lone swing, paint-chipped monkey bars, and broken see-saw, Lexi could not see anyone.

Braydon gestured towards the scout hall, and Lexi nodded, taking off in that direction.

Once they reached the hall, Lexi used both hands to open the heavy doors before peering inside the dimly lit space. She could see two small shapes huddled in the corner of the room through the dust particles hanging in the air lit by the sun from one broken window. One was a boy of eight named Peter, and the other was 6-year-old Ollie. Peter had his arm draped loosely over Ollie's shoulder, trying to comfort the distressed youngster.

"Ollie! What's wrong?" exclaimed Lexi rushing forward, her face full of concern. Ollie was one of her favourite people in Jasper's Bay. He was super shy but always cheerful and funny once he got to know you. She hadn't ever seen him cry before. "Where's your brother, Ollie?"

Ollie shrugged, taking big gulps of air as he continued to weep.

Lexi bent down and placed her hand on the young boy's knee. "It's okay, Ollie. Can I help?" she asked softly.

Ollie turned his big brown eyes to look up at Lexi, his bottom lip trembling. "Miss Rebekka said I can't join the Partisans until I do extra work for her." Big tears welled in his eyes, and he started to cry again. "But I'm so tired from gathering food this morning. And I gathered water from the creek, too. My feet hurt." He rubbed his feet with his tiny hands.

Lexi looked at Ollie's skinny legs, all scratched from the walk in the bush this morning. "It's all right, Ollie. You don't need to do any more work today. I will talk to Rebekka. She shouldn't be telling you what to do anyway." Lexi looked sideways at Braydon with fire in her eyes. Braydon's jaw was clenched.

Ollie looked up, startled, his cheeks turning pink. "No!" his eyes were wide. "Don't say anything to Miss Rebekka. She won't let me join."

"*Miss* Rebekka?"

"Yes. Miss Rebekka. She won't let me join."

"The Partisans?"

"Yes, that's her group. She said only special people can join." He pulled his knees in close to his chest and hugged them tight. "I mustn't be special enough," he wailed.

Lexi's face fell. Tears formed in the corner of her eyes. "Oh, Ollie, you *are* special. You're the one who helped us find all the bush tucker, remember?" She placed her hand gently on Ollie's slumped shoulder. "Braydon and I would be in real trouble without you!"

Ollie stopped crying and peered up at the older children. His dark, tear-filled eyes flitted between the two of them.

Braydon nodded, and Lexi gave him an encouraging smile.

Ollie wiped his nose with the back of his hand and looked towards his friend Peter who nodded as well. Ollie sat up straight. His face looked brighter, and he gave a slight nod. "Yes," he smiled. "Yes, I did, didn't I?"

"Yes, you certainly did," agreed Lexi, wiping her eyes. "Come on, you two," she said, standing and pulling Ollie to his feet. "Enough hiding in this old shed. Go out and play!" She winked at Peter and mouthed thank you to him. He gave a subtle nod.

"Let's go play with my Lego, Ollie," suggested Peter getting to his feet and scurrying to the door. "I could do with some help."

Ollie turned to Lexi and wrapped his thin arms around her waist, giving her a quick hug.

"See you, Ollie. Go have some fun."

Ollie scampered out of the shed after his friend, his tiredness forgotten.

Lexi peered around the old scout hall. A few posters describing tying knots and earning badges still lined the walls. Their corners hung down loosely, and several were ripped and faded. She wondered if Ollie had belonged to the scout group and if he missed it. Puffing out her cheeks, she turned to face Braydon.

He stood with his legs wide, and his arms folded across his chest. He glanced behind him to ensure they were alone before saying, "What do you make of that?"

"I don't know, but that's the second time we've heard about this group of Rebekka's today." Her lips pressed together. "I don't like it. It sounds very divisive." She stared at the paint peeling from the walls.

Braydon nodded, his face glum.

Clearing her throat, Lexi said. "I should probably go and talk to her." She shrugged, twisting a lock of her hair around her finger. "Maybe it's all a misunderstanding."

"Yeah, maybe," agreed Braydon, though he did not look at all convinced.

Lexi raised her eyes to the ceiling and sighed. "Come on, let's head back into town *again*." She shoved the heavy doors open with her hip. "The last thing I feel like doing right now is talking to Rebekka."

Braydon grabbed the door before it banged shut and followed her outside.

The sun was still beating down savagely. The temperature had not yet dropped below 35 degrees Celsius, making the long walk back brutal. Braydon grimaced, peering up into the blue sky.

"Would a little bit of rain be too much to ask for," he raised his hands.

Lexi patted him on the back. "Apparently, it would," she said, staring down the deserted road leading into town. She looked back over her shoulder towards the farm and the cooler bushland. "You know, you don't have to come with me. You can head back to our camp."

"No way," exclaimed Braydon shaking his head. "I want to hear what Rebekka has to say for herself. She hasn't exactly been forthcoming about much so far."

"Hmmm, well, she had better not be trying to cause trouble. She's been here for what, a whole two minutes!" Lexi kicked the dirt in front of her before retying her hair into a tight ponytail."

"Watch out, Rebekka, Lexi means business," joked Braydon, grinning at her.

"Yes, I do!" she laughed, grabbing his hand, and pulling him forward. "Come on, let's get this done."

It took a while for Braydon and Lexi to find Rebekka. Eventually, one of the other children pointed to a white, rendered house with a little wooden porch out the front. Apparently, Rebekka hadn't wanted number 43, Jason, Lexi, and Hadley's old house. She complained that it was "too far out of town" and wanted to be right in the centre of things. So, Rebekka had moved into the white rendered house once owned by eight-year-old Alice Bremer and her family and claimed it as her own. Lexi wondered where little Alice was and whether she had been allowed to remain living in the house with Rebekka or had been moved elsewhere. Lexi mentally added the question to a list of items she wanted to ask Rebekka.

As Lexi and Braydon moved closer to the house, they noticed several children, all dressed in white shirts with red stars on the sleeves, coming and going. Lexi frowned at the sight of them. *What were they doing?* She glanced sideways at Braydon before stomping towards the home.

"I don't know what's going on here, but it doesn't look as though anyone is actually doing any *town* work," she muttered. "I'm sure some of those kids were rostered to help at the farm today."

Walking to the front door, Lexi raised her fist to knock on the red wood. It looked like it had been newly painted, and she could smell the fresh paint. Pausing with her hand mid-air, Lexi stared at the door for a moment before quickly dropping it. *Maybe it would be better to go inside without announcing her presence.*

Moving her hand to the doorknob, she slowly twisted the handle and pushed open the door. Lexi cautiously peeped inside as she craned her head around the door frame, her heart thumping in her chest.

Blinking a few times, letting her eyes adjust to the light, she could see that no one was in the dimly lit passageway. She quickly scooted inside, gesturing for Braydon to follow. Butterflies fluttered around her stomach. *Why did she feel as though she was breaking and entering!* All the kids in Jasper's Bay came and went from each other's houses without an invitation or even knocking on doors. Somehow, this felt different.

Hesitating, Lexi glanced at Braydon, who was now standing close behind her. She could feel his warm breath on the back of her neck.

He placed one hand on her shoulder. "Come on. Let's find Rebekka," he whispered, pointing down the hallway.

Lexi nodded and moved forward, trying not to make the floorboards creak under her feet. She felt as though she were in a suspense movie, and her heart continued hammering like a big bass drum in her chest as she slowly crept forward.

There were two doors on either side of the passageway. Both were closed. Lexi turned her head to glance at them before deciding to keep moving. *They were probably bedrooms, and she could always return to them later.*

Seeing light emanating from a half-open doorway at the end of the long passageway to her right, Lexi continued to move forward. She kept close to the wall and edged along, her back brushing the smooth plaster as she went.

Just before she reached the doorway, Lexi paused and leaned back against the cream-coloured wall. She could hear people talking, and she tried to listen to the conversation. It sounded as though Rebekka was talking to one of the younger boys. Her voice was stern and serious.

"You know what you have to do."

"I'll try."

"Well, you'd better do more than try. I want it done today," Rebekka demanded firmly.

Lexi leaned her body closer to the doorway listening hard. The room had fallen silent. Holding her breath, she tilted her head sideways.

Suddenly Rebekka cleared her throat loudly, making Lexi jump. "You can come in, Lexi. No need to loiter outside."

Lexi's eyes widened. "What the hell!" she mouthed, turning her head towards Braydon. "How did she know I was here?"

Braydon, who had crept up behind Lexi, shrugged and shook his head.

Turning back towards the doorway, Lexi straightened her shoulders and took a deep breath before entering the window-lit room.

It was the kitchen.

Rebekka was sitting at a round, glass table and eight-year-old Liam stood beside her, his shoulders slumped. He looked nervously at Lexi as she entered the room, blinking back tears.

Lexi smiled encouragingly at him.

Dropping his eyes to the floor, Liam quickly scurried out the door. They could hear his feet slapping on the hard wooden floorboards in the passageway as he hurried to make his way outside.

As soon as Liam left the room, Lexi pulled a chair from the kitchen table and moved to sit.

"What can I do for you, Lexi?" barked Rebekka, her tone gruff. "I'm rather busy. You know, new town and everything." She drummed her fingers on the table, making a harsh clacking sound as her nails hit the glass.

Lexi paused and stood awkwardly, resting her hands on the back of the chair. She cleared her throat. "Well, Rebekka, obviously, you're new here. But you should know that we have a system in town, so everyone does a fair share of work depending upon their age." She looked at the older woman hopefully. However, Rebekka remained tight-lipped and silent.

"It's so that all the jobs that need doing get done fairly."

Rebekka continued to remain silent, her beady eyes watching Lexi.

Lexi blinked rapidly. Unsure what to say next, she pulled at the corner of her shirt and glanced towards the firmly closed window above the sink. The room felt stuffy and hot, like a heated sauna. Lexi wondered how Rebekka could stand it. Her fingers twitched wanting to open the window even if it was just a crack.

Lexi took a tiny step forward towards the window but could feel Rebekka's eyes boring into her skin, so she stopped and stood where she was.

The awkward silence continued.

Thankfully, at that moment, Braydon, who had been lingering outside, poked his head through the door and peered into the room. He took a quick look at Lexi before joining them in the kitchen. He lounged against the doorframe with his legs in front of him and his arms crossed across his chest. He didn't say anything, and Rebekka ignored him.

Lexi could feel the buzz of tension building in the room; however, she was determined to try again. She wiped her hot palms on her shorts. "Look, I'm not sure what this thing is you have going on with the white shirts, but I don't...."

"It's just a club," Rebekka interrupted. "Your sister doesn't have a problem with it."

Lexi opened her mouth, then closed it. She looked at Rebekka. "I didn't say I had a *problem* with it. I just want to make sure some of the kids are not being excluded," she said, trying to be reasonable.

Rebekka smiled at her, but her eyes remained hard. "I'm sure you have other things to worry about, Lexi," she remarked snidely, looking over at Braydon, who frowned.

She abruptly pushed her chair back from the table and walked to the kitchen counter. Slowly pouring herself a glass of water from a plastic jug, Rebekka smiled as she watched the water flow into her cup. "I've asked some of the children to do a few tasks for me," she explained sweetly, pointing to the jug. "Collecting water, making my bed, bringing me a few titbits. That type of thing." Her eyes narrowed as she turned to look at Lexi as though challenging her. "Just to help me settle in."

Lexi crossed her arms in front of her. She looked at the water jug, her eyebrows drawn together. "That's okay. I guess. But like I said, most of the kids already have jobs, such as collecting food and firewood. They don't have time to do other jobs as well." She thought about Ollie crying in the old scout hall.

"You really should get your own water," muttered Braydon from across the room, making Lexi smile.

Rebekka glanced between the two of them, her lips pursed. "I think collecting the bush food is a waste of time anyway."

Lexi blinked. "We use some of it to help control the virus," she tried to explain, her palms out in front of her.

Rebekka hmphed. "So, I've heard. But that's not *my* problem. I don't need it, and the other kids don't need it, either. So…" She finished the water in her glass and placed it upside down on the draining board. "Now, Lexi. I do have a lot to do, so maybe we can have this *little chat* another time," she suggested while shooing Braydon and Lexi out the door.

"And Lexi, maybe you should be getting your *own* supplies," she said, lifting her chin and smiling at Braydon, who scowled back at her.

Lexi opened her mouth to say something in reply, then closed it thinking better of it. Instead, she turned to leave. Looking back over her shoulder at Rebekka standing with her hands on her hips, she noticed a large mirror on the bench facing the kitchen door. Her eyes narrowed. *So, that's how she knew I was standing outside the room. Clever.*

Quickly returning down the passageway and outside, the pair hovered by the front door. Lexi raised her hand to shield her eyes from the bright sunlight. "That didn't go as well as I would have liked!" she moaned as she grabbed Braydon's hand and started to walk away from Rebekka's house. "Looks like she doesn't need any *help* settling in."

"No. She's got everything sorted, alright." Braydon kicked a small rock with his foot. "It certainly didn't take her very long."

Lexi stopped walking. "I know Rebekka's an adult and everything, but I'm still not sure about this Partisans club thing," Lexi whispered, glancing about her.

Seeing the street was empty, she sighed and let her shoulders drop, releasing the tension building between her shoulder blades. She pulled her hair tie from her ponytail and ran her fingers through her messy hair. "Maybe I've got it wrong, but it just sounds like a way for Rebekka to get the other kids to do things for her."

Her stomach clenched as she thought of Ollie and the other youngsters. *I hope Rebekka's not taking advantage of them.*

The younger children could be annoying with their constant squabbling and bickering, and even though they weren't her kin she felt responsible for them. Over the last year they had all become a large, sometimes unruly, but mostly happy family.

Braydon pulled at his damp t-shirt, the blue material sticking to his chest. He stared back at Rebekka's house for a moment before lightly placing his hand on Lexi's shoulder and turning her to face him. He scratched his stubbly chin. "Why don't we talk to Hadley about the Partisans," his face broke into a cheeky grin. "After all, she does have insider information."

"Yes!" agreed Lexi beaming at him. "She does. I wonder where she is."

Once again holding her hand to her eyes to shield the sun's intense glare, Lexi scanned the street. It was now the middle of the day, the hottest time, and she could not see another person anywhere. Everyone was inside, sheltering from the heat and humidity. Lexi looked down at her feet. Not even the common tiny black ants were about.

"Let's try Todd's house," suggested Braydon, pulling Lexi after him. "I bet Hadley's there."

"Good idea," laughed Lexi. "I bet she is."

Walking several streets from the town centre, they soon reached Todd's family home. Trying to keep to the shaded areas of the sidewalk wherever possible, Lexi placed her palms on her hot cheeks and sighed. She could feel prickling under her skin as the sun took its toll.

"There it is," she said with relief, pointing to a cream weather-board style house with a wide veranda. Braydon was right. Hadley and Todd were sitting in the shade in two oversized cane chairs. The little dog, Polo was sitting on Hadley's lap whilst she tickled him under the chin, which he seemed to be enjoying.

As Lexi and Braydon opened the little wire gate leading to Todd's yard, Polo's eyes sprung open, and he gave a happy yap, leaping from Hadley's lap and running to greet them.

"Hello, boy," exclaimed Lexi, bending down to rub his back enthusiastically. "What a good dog!" Polo's tail wagged back and forth like a car's windscreen wiper on high-speed making Lexi giggle.

"Hi!" she called, straightening. "Can we come and sit in the shade for a bit?"

"Sure," replied Todd gesturing to a couple of spare chairs. "What are you two doing wandering the streets in this heat? Your faces are bright red."

Walking up the steps of the veranda, Lexi fanned her hand in front of her face. She flumped down into one of the chairs and pointed to a jumble of cards on the table. Todd and Hadley were in the middle of a game of Uno. "Who's winning?" she asked, smiling at Hadley, who loved playing cards.

"Not me," replied Hadley, pouting. "I think Todd's cheating."

Todd laughed and winked at her. "Never!"

Hadley's face and neck flushed pink.

Lexi's eyes flicked between the pair. She twisted a lock of hair around her little finger before beginning to talk. "So, guys. We just had a little chat with Rebekka."

Hadley squirmed in her seat and kept her eyes cast down at her Uno cards.

"She was telling us about your group, *The Partisans*," continued Lexi.

Hadley frowned. "She's not supposed to do that!" Her eyes went to her sister's face. "And it's not *my* group. It's *everyone's* group."

Braydon leant back against the cream wooden balustrade. "Well, I don't think that's true, is it? It doesn't seem as though *everyone* can join."

Hadley didn't say anything. She looked back down at her cards.

"Hadley?" Lexi's voice was firm.

"Oh, alright!" steamed Hadley, throwing her cards on the table. "Yes, only a few people can join. But that's what makes it fun. And I didn't make the rules!"

Lexi picked up a card from the pile on the table and turned it over in her fingers. It was a skip your turn card. She stared at it thoughtfully before replying. "It's not much fun for the people who are left out. Especially the younger kids." She tossed the card back on the table. "We found Ollie crying in the old scout hall because he couldn't complete some tasks. What's that all about?"

Hadley picked at her fingernail, remaining silent.

"Hadley?"

"We're not supposed to say."

"Hadley! We're talking about Ollie," Lexi coaxed.

"I can't say anything!" snapped Hadley, standing, and pushing herself away from the table. Her chair tipped and fell back on the floor noisily. "Rebekka said *specifically* not to tell *you*." She looked guiltily at Lexi, who had her lips pressed tightly together.

Hadley groaned and folded her arms across her chest. "I suppose if Rebekka's already talked to you about the club, it doesn't matter anyway. I don't know why it's got to be a secret at all! It's just supposed to be a bit of fun. That's what *she* said, anyway."

"I'm not going to tell her you guys said anything," replied Lexi, going to stand by Braydon. "We'd just like to know what's happening in the town. It's not easy being stuck out there in the bush away from everyone, you know."

Hadley looked over at Todd, who nodded. He started gathering up the cards.

"Okay. What do you want to know?" Hadley took the cards from Todd and started shuffling them in her hands.

Lexi licked her lips. They felt dry. "Well, for a start, what are these tasks Ollie was talking about?" she asked before taking a small sip from her container of bush remedy.

Hadley tapped her foot on the floor. "He shouldn't have been talking about them."

"He's only a little kid, and he was upset."

Hadley nodded but didn't elaborate.

"So, Hadley, what are the tasks?" Lexi tried to coax her sister, peering intently at her.

Hadley rolled her eyes before glaring at Lexi. "It's no big deal anyway," she muttered, dropping the cards, and picking at her fingernail. She placed the edge of her finger in her mouth and chewed on the rough nail. The other three watched her remaining silent. Time ticked on.

"Oh, alright!" exclaimed Hadley rolling her eyes again. "I'll tell you!"

Hadley twisted her head and checked the street before speaking again. She lowered her voice. "To get into the Partisans, you have to complete a *mission*," she whispered.

"A mission?" asked Braydon, his eyes narrowed.

"Yeah. A mission. A task," piped up Todd, who had been noticeably quiet until now.

"And what was *your* mission, Hadley?" asked Lexi, her head tilted slightly to the side.

Hadley giggled. "Don't worry, it wasn't anything too spicy! I just had to find a big standing mirror for Rebekka's house."

Lexi put her hands in the front of her jeans pockets and nodded. "I saw it. It's a nice one."

Hadley grinned. "I got it from the JRS clothing store. Todd had to help me carry it." She picked up the remainder of the playing cards and started reshuffling them.

"What about the other kids? What are their missions?" questioned Braydon.

Hadley and Todd both shrugged.

"Dunno." Todd shook his head.

"Obviously, we don't know. We're not supposed to tell anyone our missions, remember," Hadley remarked sassily. Lexi raised her right eyebrow and scratched her nose.

Hadley stopped shuffling the cards, picked up her fallen chair and sat back down. "Look. Like I said, it was just supposed to be a bit of fun, something to do. It's exceedingly boring in this town." She stared down at her hands for a moment before looking back up at her sister. "I think some of the older boys might be taking it all too seriously, though."

Braydon who was sitting in the chair opposite Hadley, leaned forward. It creaked with his weight. "What do you mean, Hadley?"

Hadley glanced at Todd before answering. "We think some of the older boys are bullying some of the young ones for not completing the tasks or being too slow."

Lexi stepped forward, placing her hand on Hadley's shoulder. "Does Rebekka know?"

"I don't know. We saw one of the youngsters being thrown to the ground by Jakob."

Lexi nodded, frowning.

"Anyway, we tried to intervene, and he told us to mind our own business. He said he was Rebekka's personal deputy, whatever *that* means. He's got a star *and* a cross on his sleeve." She sounded a little envious.

"Hmmm. I don't think the Partisans are just a *fun* group, Hadley." Lexi steepled her fingers in front of her. "I think Rebekka has an ulterior motive."

"What? No, I don't think so," disagreed Hadley, her voice rising. "What kind of *motive*? She wouldn't do anything like that!" Hadley's face and neck flushed a mottled pink colour. "I really think the Partisans thing is just some entertainment. Rebekka is just trying to fit into the town." Hadley raised her eyebrows. "Remember what it was like when we first came here. It wasn't easy."

"No, it wasn't easy," agreed Lexi. "But we didn't try and make kids do jobs for us, did we?" She chewed on the side of her thumbnail. "I don't know. I just have a feeling she's lying about something. She still hasn't told us how come she doesn't have the virus. It's weird."

Hadley nodded; her face sheepish. "That's true." She shrugged.

Lexi sighed. Her eyes flicked to Braydon's momentarily before she rubbed them with her fingers. "I guess we'd better have *another* town meeting." She shook her head slowly. "I thought we had gotten over all this stupid bullying."

Ambling to an oversized black sofa sitting in the corner of the veranda, Lexi flumped her body into its soft folds. She closed her eyes. Her face looked strained.

Hadley joined her, perching on the edge of the sofa's arm. "Are you okay?"

Lexi slowly opened her eyes. "Not really. I haven't been sleeping well. I keep having these weird dreams."

Hadley noticed the dark bluish, black circles under her sister's eyes. "Do you think it's the virus?"

"Maybe. Braydon's been having vivid dreams too."

Hadley leaned back in the chair and stretched her arms above her head. "Listen, Lexi. Don't worry about Rebekka. She's an adult; I'm sure she knows what she's doing."

Lexi exchanged a worried glance with Braydon.

"Hmmm, yeah, well, *she* might know what she is doing, but the problem is *we* don't know what that is." Lexi took a deep breath, letting her shoulders rise and fall. She rested her chin on her hands. "Maybe we'll find out at the town meeting. Somehow, I think there are going to be a few fireworks. I'm going to need to steel myself." Lexi gazed out across the yard.

"Well, Lexi, you won't be alone," smiled Braydon, walking, and standing behind her, resting his hands on her shoulders and lightly squeezing them.

Gazing out beyond the veranda, Lexi noticed a large flock of pink and grey galahs fly by the house as they looked for shelter from the heat of the day. As Lexi watched the birds fly away, she wished she could fly away with them.

CHAPTER FIVE

The sunlight shining through the church windows lit up the dust particles floating in the air which created a warm yellow glow. Usually, this would encourage a peaceful, tranquil atmosphere; however, the little church was abuzz with unease this morning. Children murmured between themselves as they sat in tight little groups amongst the pews, their heads bent as they cast suspicious glances at each other. The tension was rife.

As Lexi pushed open the double wooden doors and walked down the aisle towards the pulpit, she took a deep breath, rolled her shoulders, and tried to relax; she needed to stay calm and focused on what she wanted to say. Giving in to her own apprehension would only fuel the situation.

Glancing back over her shoulder, Lexi could see Braydon, Hadley, and Todd following her. It gave her some comfort to know she wasn't facing the crowd alone. As if feeling her nervousness, Braydon winked at her and nodded for encouragement. Lexi nodded in return before turning and walking up the pulpit stairs.

Jason and Logan sat in one of the front pews of the church, their legs touching. Jason's left foot jiggled up and down, and Logan touched his knee to calm him. When they saw Lexi and the others enter the church, the two boys quickly stood and walked to the wooden lectern stationed at the front. Hadley and Todd took their places in the pews, and the others gathered around Lexi.

She cleared her throat and tapped on the wooden surface with a ruler as though she were a teacher about to begin a lesson. Unexpectantly, the room fell silent, and the sea of children's faces peered up at her. Some scowling, some complacent and some fearful.

Lexi scanned the small room until she found the face she was looking for. Rebekka. Rebekka was sitting very still at the rear of the building amongst a group of older children who were all wearing matching white t-shirts with red stars.

Lexi swallowed. Her throat felt dry, and she licked her lips.

"Well, thanks everyone for joining us all here this afternoon. I know you are all busy with your daily chores." She smiled encouragingly at the crowd. "I wanted to call this meeting to *officially* welcome our newest member of Jasper's Bay into the town." Lexi gestured to Rebekka with her hand. "Welcome, Rebekka. I'm sure you've managed to settle into the town alright," she smiled.

Sitting with her hands folded in her lap, Rebekka nodded slightly and returned the smile, though the smile didn't reach her eyes.

"The second thing we need to discuss is the roster Hadley has drawn up for the next two weeks. I know you all have your usual jobs, but we may have to change some around. We are running very low on firewood, and Zac says there is a major infestation of weevils in the grain we harvested last week. If anyone has any ideas on how to combat that, please see him on the Bailey farm. I know he could use some extra help."

The other children in the church began to chat amongst themselves, discussing the insect problem.

"Bailey farm?" a sharp voice called out from the rear of the room, interrupting Lexi. "Is that the farm where I first met you?"

Lexi knew who was asking the question.

"Yes, Rebekka. It's on the outskirts of town. It belongs to the Bailey family, so we call it Bailey's farm."

Lexi turned to the other children. "So, does anyone have…."

"Is that where you grow your food?" Rebekka interrupted.

Lexi knew Rebekka would have seen the small fields and fruit trees when she arrived on the farm a few days ago. She frowned, unsure why Rebekka was asking.

"Er, well, yes, most of it. We also have vegetable plots and a few fruit trees in our backyards. Plus, bush foods when we can find them. We can show…."

"That would be a good place to hide food up there," Rebekka interrupted again.

"What?"

Rebekka sat straighter. "Up on the farm away from the town and the other kids. You're not hiding food up there, are you?" she tilted her head to the side questioningly. A sly smile spread across her face as though she had discovered a secret.

A hush fell over the crowded little room. It suddenly felt hot and stifling inside, and Lexi pulled at the collar of her blouse. Her fingers brushed the lid of the flask tied to the belt of her shorts. The container held a fresh brew of bush remedy.

"No, why would we do something like that!" she replied. Her voice was high with indignation. She looked out at the children sitting in front of her. Some children looked confused, some frowning, and some glared at her in suspicion. They whispered to each other behind their hands.

Her face grew flushed in anger. Hadley and Lexi had been part of the town of Jasper's Bay for a year. The children all knew them and welcomed them into their town. Or at least that's what she had thought. She clenched her teeth, trying to quell the virus-fuelled anger growing in her belly.

A twittering laugh sounded from the back of the room. "Only joking, Lexi," winked Rebekka. "It would be a nice part of town to live, though. A nice easy life with all that food so close by."

Lexi's mouth dropped open. *Was Rebekka purposefully trying to create disruption?* She took a deep breath and was about to reply when Zac stood from the middle of the room and turned to face Rebekka. His head was still bandaged from the altercation he had with his brother Kevin. He was a little unsteady on his feet, clutching the pew in front of him for support.

"I'm Zac Bailey. It's my family farm. And for your information, there's not much food and a lot of bloody hard work. Tending to a farm is as far away from easy as you can get," Zac glared at Rebekka. "And as you seem so interested, we can't use the seeder or tractor because we don't have any fuel. We planted, watered, and harvested all the crops you see by hand." He rubbed his palm across his forehead, his voice firm. "It all takes a long time, and everything we grow, we share." Zac turned to face Lexi, nodded his head to her and flopped back down in his seat.

Many of the children in the church looked on suspiciously.

"Thank you, Zac. You've all worked on the farm," argued Lexi, her hands splayed out in front of her. "Except for the hay and seed for the animals, you all *know* there isn't any extra food stored on there. Everything gets brought to town and shared equally." Lexi looked back at Braydon, Jason, and Logan. Her mouth felt dry. This wasn't how she wanted the meeting to start.

Jason shook his head, and Logan shrugged. They looked as perplexed as she felt. Braydon just looked angry. His face was red, his hand tapping his thigh repeatedly.

Lexi blew out a slow breath as she tucked her hair behind her ears. She again turned to face the crowd. "So, one of the reasons I called this meeting is I think we should discuss the formation of the *Partisans*. I think…"

"It's a *private* group," Rebekka called out, interrupting once again.

"Well, yes, that's part of the issue." Lexi could feel the tension growing between her shoulders and a trickle of sweat rolled down her spine. "I don't think it's a good idea to have a group that only some people can join."

The noise level in the church suddenly rose as children started to talk over the top of each other. Lexi raised her voice trying to be heard over the ruckus. "We need to work together. Be united. It's hard enough already."

No one was listening to her. Even Braydon, Jason and Logan were talking amongst themselves. Only one face was turned towards her. Rebekka's. And she was smiling.

Several of the kids in white shirts stood. With their feet splayed apart, and their arms folded angrily across their chests they scowled at her. Lexi could feel their anger flowing towards her like daggers and she felt her fingers curl into tight fists at her sides. Her stomach started to churn.

One of the kids in white shirts yelled out, "you can't tell us what to do!" His voice cracked with emotion.

Lexi thought it sounded like Aiden, a boy she had helped only last week when he had fallen from his BMX bike and scrapped all the skin from his shins. Her shoulders slumped. *What was going on here?*

"You don't even belong here!" Another called out viciously.

Someone from the crowd in front of her gasped. Lexi looked down searchingly and realised it was Hadley. Their eyes met in dismay. "Why are they so angry?" mouthed Hadley. Lexi shrugged. Her hands were beginning to shake.

"Okay, boys," chirped Rebekka smiling at them indulgently. She gestured with her hands for them to sit down before striding purposefully toward the front of the pulpit.

Lexi had begun to quiver all over with rage. Braydon and Jason had grabbed her hands, trying to calm her, while Braydon whispered soothingly in her ear. But Lexi was focused entirely on Rebekka, who was marching towards her like an officer in the army.

"I think I'll take it from here, Lexi," Rebekka cooed sweetly. "I think you had better have a *rest*." She cast her eyes over Lexi, slowly looking her up and down with disdain. You seem pretty *emotional*."

Lexi felt her cheeks flame scarlet and her fists clenched even tighter until the knuckles were white.

Standing next to Lexi, Rebekka smiled at the children seated in front of her as though they were a class of students, and she was their teacher. "Lexi is going to have a little *rest* outside." She picked a bit of fluff from her shirt sleeve and flicked it on the floor. "Like Zac said, it's hard work growing food. We must make sure *everyone* is fit enough to do their share."

Rebekka's eyes followed Lexi down the church aisle as Jason and Braydon hurried her outside and away from the others. Angry voices followed them all the way down the aisle and outside.

"What the hell!" exclaimed Lexi as soon as they exited the church. She began pacing back and forth in front of the heavy wooden door, now firmly closed. Lexi was fuming, her nostrils flaring.

Braydon didn't hesitate. He took two quick strides towards her and grabbed Lexi's hand, forcing her to stop. "Here," he said, raising his flask to her mouth. "You need to drink this," his voice was on edge.

Lexi glared at the flask. "*You,* need to drink it!" she retorted, pushing it away.

"I will," he said, giving her a crooked smile. "After you. Having a meltdown is not going to help."

"I'm not having a meltdown!" she yelled. "And anyway, it might make me feel a lot better!"

Braydon took her hand and squeezed it. "No, it won't. You'll regret it later."

"He's right," piped up Jason, standing with his arms hanging by his side. His usual chipper face looked crestfallen. "It will only turn them against you even more." He nodded his head towards the church door.

Lexi sighed. She looked at the little church standing before her, picturing the children inside with their angry and scared faces glaring at her. She took a long drink from Braydon's flask, wiped her mouth with the back of her hand and passed the flask to Braydon. "But that's just it. I don't understand why they are so angry at me. I haven't *done* anything."

"I think this Partisan group thing is leaving everyone unsettled and confused. They're just lashing out," suggested Jason as he tried to peer through one of the churches' stained glass windows.

Just then, one of the big doors started to open, and Hadley poked her head out. She pushed the door open and came outside, quickly closing it behind her. Her head swung back and forth, taking in the situation. Spotting Lexi, she ran to her sister and hugged her tightly. "Are you alright?" she released her and looked at her face. "What the heck just happened!?"

Placing her hands on her knees, Lexi breathed deeply, trying to steady herself. She gave a nervous laugh. "I don't know. And no, I'm not alright."

Hadley looked at her sister in concern; her forehead was crumpled with worry lines. "Come on," she said, grabbing at Lexi's arm. "Let's get you away from everyone for a bit."

Lexi straightened and placed her hot hand over Hadley's. It's okay, Hadley. I need you to stay here."

Hadley's eyes dropped to the floor in disappointment, as if she weren't needed.

"I need you to go back in there and be my eyes and ears," said Lexi grabbing Hadley's hands in hers. She could feel the bush tonic starting to work. Her heartbeat had begun to slow down, and the pounding in her head had subdued to a dull thud.

"Listen, Hadley. I don't know what just happened in there, but I have a feeling that *Miss* Rebekka is very pleased with herself right now." Lexi looked towards the closed church doors. "You need to go back in there and find out what's happening. We can't let this town implode."

Brushing the hair from her eyes, Hadley looked at her solemnly. "I'm sure Rebekka didn't mean what she said. She just doesn't know how we do things."

Lexi rubbed at her bloodshot eyes. "Okay, Hadley." She sighed, not wanting to argue. Her hands were beginning to shake again. She could feel them against her skin. "Can you please just go back in and find out what's going on," her voice wobbled. "I can't go back in there. Not right now."

Straightening her shoulders, Hadley nodded. "Sure, Lexi. I can do that, but I'm sure Miss Rebekka was only joking with you." She walked back towards the church. Placing her hand on the big wooden door, she turned her head towards Lexi. "You should go and have a *little rest*."

Lexi tilted her head to the side and stared at Hadley's back as she entered the church. *Had she imagined it, or did Hadley just sound eerily like Rebekka?*

CHAPTER SIX

Lexi placed another log on their small campfire, watching as the red-hot flames shot orange embers into the sky. She held her hands out in front of her flexing her fingers wide. The heat from the fire was intense, just as her feelings had been back in the church only a few hours before.

How had all this drama happened? Her life, whilst always busy, was becoming hectic. For some reason unknown to Lexi, it seemed as though Rebekka was intent on causing unrest, and somehow Lexi had been caught up in the middle of it all. And being in the middle of drama was not somewhere someone with the KV17 virus wanted to be. Lexi was already having difficulty keeping control of her erratic, volatile emotions without the children of Jasper's Bay heckling and jeering at her making her feel like a troublesome outsider.

After leaving the church, Braydon and Lexi had returned to their small bush camp to be away from the rest of the children, especially Rebekka, while Lexi regained her composure. She had felt the effects of the virus sparking her anger and sending irrational thoughts into her mind. Her skin had burned and prickled as the rage grew. If Jason and Braydon had not forced her from the church, who knows how out of control the fire within her would have become.

Lexi sighed. She knew she had been complacent in taking the bush remedy of late, and without it, her control of the virus was starting to slip. She peered into the big pot cooking on the campfire containing a fresh batch of bush brew, the concoction slowly simmering on the heat. A fragrant herbal aroma filled the air. Lexi leaned forward, stirring the liquid inside, breathing in the lovely smell.

"I'd forgotten how reliant we are on this stuff," she said, her mouth turned downwards. She tapped the metal ladle on the side of the pot. "You know, I've been thinking," she looked up to make sure Braydon was listening. "We should really start learning how to dry these native herbs and store them. You know, preserve them."

"That's a good idea," agreed Braydon coming to sit by Lexi. He placed his hand on her thigh. "You never know when we might run out of the fresh ones. I have no idea if they flower all year round or not."

Lexi looked at Braydon. "Me neither." She could feel the heat of his hand through the leg of her pants. It made her skin tingle. She placed her palm over his. "Plus, you know some older kids will need it soon, too. Jason turns seventeen next month, and so does Jakob."

Braydon nodded, staring into the pot. "We're going to need to increase our supply." He pointed at the brew with a stick. "That's not going to be enough for all of us."

Lexi turned her gaze to the bushland in front of their little camp. A black fly buzzed incessantly around her face, and she shooed it away with her hand. "I wonder if we can grow some of the native plants ourselves in this area," she suggested, pointing to the bushland. "We would have to clear the area a bit. We could remove some of the undergrowth and other bushes." She chewed on her thumbnail, deep in thought. "It would be a big task, but if it worked, at least we wouldn't have to forage for supplies. They'd all be in the one spot," she smiled. "It will be our little bush medicine grove."

Braydon peered into the thick bush where Lexi was suggesting. "It will take a while for the plants to grow, and we're probably going to have to use seeds." He frowned and scratched his nose. "I don't think native plants take too kindly to being dug up and replanted. And we would have to hand water them."

Lexi stood and moved closer to the bush. She stretched her arms above her head. "Yes, I know. I didn't say it would be easy, but we should start planning for the future. This virus isn't going away. We need to continue to learn to control it." Lexi turned her head back towards Braydon. "You know, I don't think the other kids in town have really thought about it. It still seems a long way off for them, but eventually, as they get older, they will have to learn to control it too. No one is going to find a cure for us."

Bending forward, Lexi rubbed some tiny fragrant leaves from a brown and yellow Boronia bush between her fingers. She brought the leaves to her face and breathed in the delightful fragrance. "I'm going to add seed gathering and drying the fruits and herbs to our list of chores," she proposed, her face determined. "I know everyone is super busy and will probably whine about it, but I think it's important."

Lexi walked back to the fire and used a large tree branch to hook under the handle of the boiling pot of herbs. Using two hands on the branch, she carefully removed it from the flames to cool. "I'm not ready to give into this virus."

Braydon chuckled, standing and placing his arms around Lexi's shoulders. "Me neither," he said, pulling her close to him. "I'll help you clear the bushland." He buried his face in her hair. "But let's start tomorrow. After what happened in the church, I don't think now is a good time to bring up extra duties. Especially ones regarding *our* remedy."

Lexi nodded glumly, thinking about what had occurred back in the church. "Yeah, fair enough," she agreed. "It won't be *only* for us much longer, though, will it. The sooner they understand that the better for them."

Braydon stroked Lexi's tangled hair. "You know Jason and Jakob will probably want to move out here with us, away from the town, soon."

Turning to face him, Lexi looked into Braydon's blue eyes. "Logan won't like that," she smiled, thinking of their friends.

"He's not the only one," remarked Braydon touching Lexi's face gently. "It's going to get very crowded here pretty soon," he said, his eyes twinkling.

Lexi looked at Braydon's lips, and her heart skipped. She could feel the heat radiating between their bodies and she leaned in closer to him, her lips softly brushing his. She closed her eyes for a moment before pulling back away from him. Her lips tingled.

Looking up at him through her eyelashes, Lexi was unsure how he felt. They'd become close, but did he want to take it any further? She let out a breath when she saw he was smiling. A big cheeky grin was spread across his face.

Lexi knew with the virus coursing through their veins, it was a risk to intentionally or non-intentionally increase their emotions, but she couldn't help herself. With the future so uncertain, some risks were worth taking. She took his warm hand in hers, their fingers entwining. Her other hand lightly brushed the coarse stubble on his cheek with her fingers before she once again leaned into him and kissed him firmly on the lips. If their little sanctuary was going to become a whole lot more crowded, then she was going to make the most of their isolation whilst she could.

Back in the centre of town, Jakob, Aiden, and Das were cramming food items into a cardboard box. All three had their heads together, whispering. Their movements were quick as they continually glanced around.

"I think someone's coming," remarked Das standing tall and dropping his hands to his sides.

"Doesn't matter," sneered Jakob. "I'm on duty in here today anyway. I'm supposed to be in here."

Aiden and Das glanced sideways at each other. "Well, we're not!" they chorused together.

Jakob shook his head. "Relax," he smirked. "No one is going to say anything." He looked towards the box they had been filling with food items. "Better put that under the counter," he suggested tapping the box with his finger.

Just as Aiden was stashing the box of food under the counter, the door to the front of the old shop opened, and a little bell tinkled somewhere in one of the back rooms. Aiden pushed the box further in with the toe of his shoe.

The children of Jasper's Bay had set up a food storage area in an old delicatessen in the town centre. None of the fridges or cool rooms worked anymore; however, the shelves and counters were useful for storing food. All food collected from the Bailey farm, fruit trees and bush foods were stored here for equal distribution amongst the town kids. Each of the older children took it, in turn, to work in the supply centre and distribute the daily food rations. There were usually two children on at a time.

"Hey," chimed Jessica, a fifteen-year-old girl with short blonde hair. "You're here early!" she said, smiling at Jakob. "You usually hate this job." She laughed, placing a box of corn and apples from the farm onto one of the empty shelves.

Jakob shrugged, his face blank. "Just wanted to get a head start. These two wanted to help." He suggested jerking his thumb towards his two friends.

"Oh." Jessica looked surprised. "I think four people in here is going to be too many." She frowned. "There's not much to do, really."

Jakob, Aiden, and Das looked awkwardly at each other.

Jakob forced a laugh. "She's right. You guys go. You can help me with that other stuff later."

Das nodded.

"What other stuff?" asked Jessica. "I can help if you want."

Jakob laughed again. He rubbed his chin. "Ahh, no, that's alright. It's just a little project I have."

The brass bell above the door tinkled again as one of the younger kids walked in, ready to collect the food ration for his house. Das and Aiden quickly scooted out the open door.

"Hi, Michael," said Jessica warmly, waving her hand at the young boy in a blue Wiggles shirt. "What have you been up to?"

Michael shrugged. He cast a worried glance at Jakob.

Jakob pulled a clipboard from the shelf behind him and placed it on the counter. The clipboard contained a list of all the children in town and their houses. He slowly ran his finger down the list.

He stopped when he reached Michael's name and tapped his finger. "Hmm, so you have four kids living together in your house?"

Michael nodded.

"But I see only one of them, Billy, is a member of the Partisans. So, that means you only get *one* full ration and three half rations."

Michael's mouth dropped open.

Jessica's head swung to look at Jakob. She frowned. "What are you talking about, Jakob? What do you mean they get *half* shares?"

Jakob looked bored. He sighed. "They're not one of the Partisans, so they only get a half share of rations. Only Partisans get a full ration," he explained, speaking slowly as if to a young child.

Jessica stared at him. "I don't know anything about this."

Jakob turned to face her. He put his hands on his hips and puffed out his chest as if expecting trouble. "It's a new rule, Jessica. Only Partisans get a full ration."

He turned back to face Michael whose chin was trembling.

"Look. If you want extra food, you have to join the Partisans or do extra work for us."

"Wait," said Jessica placing her hand on Jakob's arm. "How come I don't know anything about this?" she looked confused.

Jakob groaned. "Jessica, you're not part of the Partisans, are you? So, you wouldn't know. I'm telling you now. Rebekka made the new rule."

"Rebekka?"

"Yes, Rebekka." He turned again to Michael and angrily stuffed a few items into the boy's cloth bag. "Here," he said, thrusting the bag at the young boy standing with his thin arms hanging limply by his sides. "Take these or don't have anything. Your choice."

Michael flinched. His small hand reached up and quickly grabbed the half-empty bag. He glanced sideways at Jessica before turning and scrambling out the door.

"What do you mean *extra* chores?" enquired Jessica running her hand through her short, cropped hair.

Jakob smirked. "Bringing Rebekka things she needs, cleaning her house, helping us with some of *our* chores," he shrugged.

Jessica crossed her arms in front of her chest. "And who decided on these new rules."

"I told you. Rebekka did."

"Rebekka? Not the council?"

"Yes, Rebekka." Jakob smiled. A big grin stretched across his face. He stared at Jessica with narrowed eyes.

"Can she do that?" Jessica continued to frown.

"Well, she's an adult, isn't she?"

Jessica returned Jakob's stare momentarily before dropping her gaze to the floor. She reached across, grabbed the clipboard, and scanned the listed names. Several on each page had red stars next to them. The emblem of the Partisans. Hers wasn't one of them.

Dropping the clipboard back onto the counter, Jessica turned to stare at the collection of food supplies behind them, unsure of what to do.

"But what does Lexi have to say about these new rules?" she asked uncertainly.

"Lexi," Jakob snorted. "What has Lexi got to do with it?"

"Well…" stammered Jessica turning to face him. "The thing is, she did start the council and everything. Remember how disorganised we were before."

"Yeah, well, like I said. We've got an adult here now." Jakob stared at Jessica with a sneer on his face. "Rebekka is going to be doing the *organising* now."

Jessica stared at Jakob, her eyes narrowing. She opened her mouth as if to say something further before slowly returning to face the shelves. Her hand rested on one of the tins of food before Jessica slowly started to straighten the boxes and rows of fruit while Jakob smirked and laughed under his breath.

Over in the main square, the sound of hammering and sawing could be heard, echoing through the quiet streets. Planks of wood, long nails, and tools had been strewn around haphazardly. The town centre had become a building site.

Aiden, Das, and a few other boys were busily building a structure in the middle of the paved quadrangle. Several paving stones had been removed, and a hole dug down deep in the sandy area. A long wooden beam was sticking out from the pit, standing upright, and stretching to the sky.

Aiden was slouching with his hands on his hips, staring up at it. "I think it's too tall," he complained, looking over at the others.

Das stopped sawing his piece of wood and came over to join him. "It doesn't matter how tall that piece is," he said. It's the horizontal pieces that matter. We have to get them right, or it won't work."

Aiden looked up and down at the wood before nodding in agreement. Then, bending over to retrieve his shovel, he started digging another hole about one and a half meters from the first.

It didn't take him long, and once the hole was dug and a second long plank of wood was placed inside, Aiden stood back to admire his handiwork. One of the poles tilted slightly to the left, so he stomped his foot down on the earth to straighten and secure it. He drew the back of his hand across his sweaty brow before wiping it on his shorts. "Mr Mathews would be so proud of us." He chuckled. "I always loved woodwork class."

Das looked up from where he had been sawing a half-moon shape in a flat plank of wood. "Yeah, me too, mate. Much better than English or maths class!"

Aiden plucked at his white shirt with the red star on its sleeve. The material, now a dirty grey colour, clung to his sweaty chest. "God, that's one thing I DO NOT MISS. Going to school and having to listen to the teachers droning on and on."

Das laughed, hiking his loose shorts up. "I don't care if I never have to read another poem ever again. Boring!"

Aiden laughed too before his eyes flicked towards a group of younger kids who had gathered around a large wire structure set up in the corner of the quadrangle. Their fingers gripped the wire as they stared wistfully at the contents inside. A large brass padlock held the two doors firmly together.

"Hey!" yelled Aiden throwing a piece of wood towards them. "Get away from there!"

The children yelped and jumped back as the piece of wood skittered across the ground and hit the container with a loud bang making it shake. The wire container contained an assortment of bikes, skateboards, balls, and other toys.

The younger children turned to stare at Aiden and Das. One of the braver of the group called out. "Can we have them back? Pleeese."

Aiden put his hands to his eyes. "You know the rules. You can have them back when you agree to do the extra work, we set you."

One of the younger children started to cry. "It's too hard. We can't do it!" His lip trembled, and fat tears rolled down his cheeks.

Das smirked. "Stupid little kids."

"Crying's not going to help," barked Aiden gruffly. "Go and do the extra work we set you, or you're never getting your stuff back." His voice was hard and firm.

The younger children stood and stared at him for a few moments before turning and running away, tears streaming down their faces.

Aiden watched them leave before shaking his head. He started hammering a metal hinge into a flat rectangle of wood. The plank of wood had a semi-circle shape cut from its middle and matched up flawlessly when placed above another board. He stood back with his hands shoved into his jean's pockets and grinned. It looked perfect. "Miss Rebekka is gonna love this!" he exclaimed cheerfully; his eyes gleaming.

Das agreed. "Looks like a giant packman," he laughed, opening and closing the two pieces now hinged together. "Let's connect them to the pole, and we're done. She's gonna be surprised we got it done so quickly."

"Yeah, well, like I said before. I *am* good at woodwork," smirked Aiden, brushing his sweaty lank hair from his eyes.

"Yeah, but not much else," teased Das, punching Aiden on the arm.

Aiden swiftly punched Das back before kicking his legs out from under him. The two dropped their tools to the ground and began wrestling in the red dirt, getting their white Partisan shirts even dirtier.

It was now very late in the afternoon, and Lexi's feet dragged. She had once again made the long walk from her camp back into town to talk to Rebekka. A light breeze rustled the green leaves of the eucalyptus trees that lined the old road leading into Jasper's

Bay, and she tilted her head, feeling the cool relief on her cheeks. Even though she had been wearing a hat, the constant trudging back and forth to town in the summer heat had brought the beginnings of a pink sunburn on her face and a few more freckles.

Braydon had decided to stay back at their bush camp and bottle the cooling, fresh batch of bush brew. So, Lexi was making the journey solo, relentlessly walking one foot in front of the other down the long, straight, dusty road.

As she grew closer to reaching Rebekka's house, Lexi stopped at the edge of the town square and sat on one of the wooden benches positioned around its border. She leaned forward and tugged at her left shoe, slowly removing it from her foot. Rubbing her sore toes, she flinched as her fingers brushed the littlest one. Flexing her toes in and out, she slowly and carefully removed her sock.

As the air hit her feet, she felt a sharp sting making her grimace. Bending to examine her feet, she saw a big, white blister on the side of her little toe that had burst, leaving a flap of white skin over a very nasty red, raw patch of flesh. She grimaced, "That's going to need a Band-Aid."

As she picked at her toe, the sudden sound of yelling caught her attention. Two boys were fighting in the square. They were too far away for her to see clearly, and she wondered if she should go and intervene. Lexi wiggled her sore toes, feeling the sting with every movement.

"They can sort themselves out," she muttered to herself. The children in town were constantly squabbling over one thing or another, and she was tired of being the peacemaker. Besides, she had a bigger problem to sort out, and the less walking she did, the better. She winced as she eased her black Converse sneaker back onto her throbbing foot. She would prefer to go barefoot; however, the ground was too hot to go without shoes, even this late in the day. Only overnight would it cool down.

Hobbling, Lexi slowly grew nearer to Rebekka's white-rendered house. She puffed out her cheeks and slowly released the air tapping the fresh flask of bush remedy hanging from her pants belt with her fingers. The metal made a clinking sound underneath her fingernails.

As she stood outside Rebekka's house, Lexi stared at the freshly painted red door and shook her head. It was the only newly painted door in the whole of Jasper's Bay and not a priority when there was plenty of firewood to collect, rubbish to burn and food to harvest. Lexi's fingers reached for her flask and took a long drink of the fragrant concoction. It was room temperature, so not particularly thirst-quenching; however, it helped quench other needs. Re-buckling the flask to her belt, she pulled her shoulders back and breathed another deep settling breath before walking briskly to the red door. Her face was determined.

"What do *you* want, Lexi?" sneered a boy of about fourteen standing by the front door. He leant back on the wooden frame and crossed his feet in front of him.

Lexi tilted her head and stared at him for a moment. "Get out of the way, Mathew. I'm here to talk to Rebekka, *not you*," she challenged, pushing past him.

Mathew laughed, giving a dramatic bow. "She's in the kitchen."

Lexi ignored him and continued walking down the same dim passageway she had been in only that morning. Running her fingers along the smooth wall, she took her time. *Was Rebekka watching her in the mirror?*

As Lexi approached the kitchen, a young boy named Giles suddenly emerged from the doorway. He nodded his head towards the open room. "Miss Rebekka is ready for you, Lexi. You can go in."

Lexi frowned. "*Miss* Rebekka," she muttered. "I am not calling her bloody *Miss* Rebekka. She's not our teacher." She hovered outside the doorway biting at a hangnail on the side of her thumb, making it bleed. With the sudden pain, she looked down at her finger in surprise before popping it in her mouth.

"She's just a person like you," Lexi whispered as she smoothed down her hair. She wiped her palms on her pants and stepped into the kitchen.

Rebekka was standing by the window. "Feeling better, Lexi?" Rebekka smiled. "You seemed upset in the church."

Lexi's face turned crimson like a bright red cherry. She stood awkwardly in the centre of the room, her arms hanging loosely by her sides. A dying fly buzzed loudly in the kitchen sink.

Rebekka turned up her nose at the sound and poured a glass of water over the insect, flushing it down the kitchen drain. Lexi stared at the wasted fresh water flowing down the sink.

"I can't stand creatures lingering around when they've outlived their welcome," Rebekka sneered before turning and impatiently pointing her finger at Lexi, gesturing for her to sit in one of the chairs surrounding the small wooden kitchen table. "What can I do for you, Lexi? You look concerned." Her voice was brisk.

Lexi took her time walking to the table before sitting perched on the edge of one of the chairs. She cleared her throat once more before looking Rebekka in the eye. "I *am* concerned, Rebekka. I don't understand what you're trying to do to our town." She tapped her foot. "We had it running nicely and efficiently, and now you are causing all this unhappiness and unrest."

Rebekka crossed her arms across her chest. She moved closer to where Lexi sat, looming over her. "Well, Lexi. It is not *your* town, though, is it? You are an outsider like me."

Lexi's mouth dropped open. "I've been here for over a year, and I didn't say it was *my* town."

Rebekka picked at a loose thread on her top before looking back at Lexi. "Hmmm. I think *since* you've been here, you have this town running just how *you* want it," Rebekka said smugly.

"I'm only a small part of this town," Lexi's voice shook angrily. "*All* the kids here decide on what happens in Jasper's Bay."

"Do they?"

Lexi's jaw tensed. "Yes, they do. We have a council to help implement the decisions."

"That's right. You have a council. And you're on this council, aren't you, Lexi."

Lexi pressed her lips together tightly for a moment before replying. She looked at Rebekka with a hard glare. "I was asked to go on the council because I'm one of the older children in town," she tried to explain. "We all vote on the rules here."

Rebekka unfolded her arms and drummed her long fingernails on the kitchen table. She watched Lexi.

Lexi glared back at her, remaining silent.

"There *are* a lot of younger children in Jasper's Bay, aren't there?" Rebekka stated. "And younger children *do* need some guidance and rules."

Lexi nodded. "Yes. But not bullying."

Rebekka's mouth turned up at one side. "They need *encouragement* to get things done. Don't you agree?"

Lexi frowned, her eyebrows coming together. "We were *already* getting things done before you arrived."

"I don't think so; just ask Zac."

Lexi looked up sharply. "What do you mean?" her voice cracked.

Rebekka turned to stare out the window. "For a start, he is not working hard enough on his farm."

Lexi blinked rapidly. "You're wrong. All he *does* is work on that farm," her voice rose emotionally. "Plus, he is recovering from a head injury and getting over the death of his twin sister!" She bit her lip, having said too much.

Rebekka clicked her tongue. "That may be, but I don't think he has the right attitude. He wouldn't let us slaughter one of his cows. As if they're his anyway." She turned her head to look back at Lexi. Her eyes were hard.

Lexi's mouth dropped open. "They *are* his cows," she snapped. "And he knows how to look after them." She shook her head, trying to explain. "We only have a few left, so we're trying to breed them. We use them for milk, not meat."

Rebekka walked to the counter and poured herself another cup of water from her plastic jug. She drank it slowly, not offering any to Lexi. "I'm sure he will change his mind soon enough," she said cryptically, peering at Lexi over the cup's rim.

"Why?" Lexi swallowed, her throat tightening.

Rebekka laughed harshly before taking another slow sip of water.

"What have you done!?" asked Lexi, her voice hard and her eyes ablaze.

Rebekka slowly placed the plastic cup back on the bench. "Let's just say he's spending some time contemplating his behaviour," she smirked.

"What does that mean?" Lexi's voice rose. "Where is he?" she demanded through clenched teeth.

"He's in the town square."

CHAPTER SEVEN

Running outside, Lexi flung the front door wide, slamming it into the wall.

"Hey!" yelled Mathew as she shoved past him.

Ignoring the pimply-faced boy, Lexi instead turned towards the direction of the town square. *What did Rebekka mean when she said Zac was contemplating his behaviour?* She placed her hand on her neck, as bile burnt her throat.

Trying to block the pain from her blistered toes, Lexi forced herself to hobble faster. The late afternoon had turned into early evening, and darkness was starting to fall. Without a torch it would be difficult to see what was going on, not to mention navigating the streets in the pitch black. There wasn't a moon out tonight, and without streetlights or house lights, the town became one giant black hole once the sun set.

As she made her way towards the square, Lexi suddenly remembered seeing the two boys fighting earlier. She hadn't paid that much attention to them as the kids in town were always fighting or disagreeing on one thing or another. *Could one of them have been Zac?*

Lexi narrowed her eyes as she saw a small group gathered by what looked like a wooden structure. She stopped and stared. *When had that been erected?*

Cautiously walking forward, Lexi approached the group. She flexed and clenched her fists, feeling uneasy. Her palms were hot and sweaty. As she kept her eyes on the group, she saw Jakob lean to one side, which gave her a better view of the structure. She frowned. It looked like one of those punishment devices used in the medieval days. They were usually placed in public places and used to shame people. The poor victim was put in the contraption and left standing bent over with their head and hands placed through holes in the wood. People watching from the crowd often threw rotten fruit and vegetables at them.

It seemed as though Jasper's Bay now had its own version of "The Stocks" and its first victim firmly confined in them. It was a boy with black hair. His feet were splayed and hanging limp on the ground. His head hung low, and his arms were floppy. Lexi couldn't see who the boy was from her current position though her stomach had a sinking feeling. Stepping to the side to gain a better view, she exhaled in a rush. It was as she feared. The boy in the stocks was Zac!

Lexi's jaw tightened as she saw the state her friend was in. One eye was swollen shut, and the top of his lip was bruised and bleeding. Zac's knees were bent as his body hung unresponsive. His arms were stretched before him, and his head drooped forward, hanging like an unwanted puppet. The white bandages from his head lay in a pile on the ground in front of him. Looming over Zac, Jakob and Aiden stood on either side of him, their hands firmly on their hips.

Watching the scene before her, Lexi could feel the heat growing in her veins. Her cheeks burned in a fury. *How dare they!* Zac was a council member and an essential part of the community. Without Zac and his family's farm, the town would have starved.

"What the hell are you doing!" she yelled at Jakob with two hands on his arm as she pushed him out of the way. Lexi stormed towards the stocks with her jaw pushed forward determinedly. The other children moved out of the way to let her through.

As she reached Zac, Lexi leaned in close and cautiously lifted his head. There was congealed blood from a cut above his swollen eye, and his mouth dropped open slackly. A thin dribble of spit fell to the ground, and he moaned in discomfort.

Lexi slowly lowered his head before straightening up and examining the wooden contraption which held him fast. His head and arms were held firmly within small circles carved into a rectangle of wood. *How did this thing open?*

With the sun starting to set and darkness beginning to form, Lexi quickly leaned in even closer, looking for a latch or some way of opening the top. To her relief, she spotted what looked like a hinge and a sliding bolt on one side of the wooden frame. She smiled and placed her hand on the bolt, ready to slide it across.

"I wouldn't do that if I were you," warned Jakob.

Lexi's hand froze. She swivelled to face Jakob. The three boys on guard were all standing, watching her intently.

"You used to go to school with Zac, remember," she hissed through gritted teeth. "Jakob, weren't you on the same football team? I thought you were friends!"

Jakob dropped his head and looked away, unable to meet Lexi's eyes. Even in the darkening gloom, she could see his cheeks had turned a deep shade of red.

Staring at him, Lexi shook her head before reaching for the bolt. This time no one said anything, so she quickly slid it across. As she placed her hand on the uppermost part of the wood, ready to lift the top, a firm hand grabbed her wrist and wrenched it away. Aiden was standing close to Lexi, glaring at her. She could smell his sweat and stale breath radiating towards her. She shrugged him off.

"This is barbaric!" she yelled in his face, her eyes wide and furious. "We don't do this to each other." She turned to face the other children who had remained watching. "And you lot should have done something to stop this!"

Lexi's shoulders slumped. Not one person said a word; they simply turned their backs and started walking away back home. She stared after them in disbelief. *they care what happened in their town, or had fear driven them away?*

With a loud sigh, Lexi turned her focus back towards Zac. As her fingers once again reached towards the rough wood, she suddenly felt a firm grip take her arm. The fingers dug into her flesh painfully.

"Aiden…: she exclaimed in frustration as the grip spun her around. Her jaw dropped open in surprise when she saw the person holding her was not Aiden but Rebekka. Lexi hadn't heard her approach.

"Rebekka?" exclaimed Lexi before a sharp crack and sting of pain broke her focus. Rebekka had just slapped her!

Tears formed in the corner of Lexi's eyes, and she raised her palm to her stinging, red cheek. Aiden and Jakob watched on, their mouths open and eyes wide. However, they remained silent and still.

"Snap out of it, you two!" growled Rebekka clicking her fingers. "Take that useless boy out of the stocks and put *her* in there." She gestured to Lexi with her finger, then turned to face the few remaining children who had stayed. "And you lot go home!"

One or two children hesitated before a loud "NOW!" sent them scurrying away.

Das, who had been standing silently over to the side, moved forward and carefully lifted Zac from the stocks. He lay the still unconscious boy on the ground.

"Lay him on his side, you idiot," yelled Lexi as she struggled with Aiden and Jakob, who held her arms as she tried to break free.

Das carefully turned Zac onto his side. He glanced at Rebekka, who wasn't watching and quickly placed a rolled-up sweater under Zac's head. "Sorry, mate," he whispered, bending close to his ear.

"Das!" ordered Rebekka in a firm voice. "Come and close the top."

Aiden and Jakob were busy trying to manoeuvre Lexi's head and arms into the small holes of the stocks, and she wasn't making it easy for them.

As she pushed and pulled against the boys, Lexi could feel the rage and anger starting to burn in the pit of her stomach, boiling to the surface as though she were a witch's cauldron. She yelled in fury at being held, and her fingers scrapped down the side of Jakob's face as she momentarily managed to brake one hand free. Jakob yelped in surprise as thin red welts formed on his cheek. As Lexi glared at him, he abruptly grabbed hold of her arm, before roughly slamming it into the hole, her wrist hitting the hard wood painfully.

"Don't do this!" yelled Lexi, but the boys refused to listen. She tried to use all her might to push against the solid wood of the stocks as it bit into her skin, and she felt the boys loosen their grip a little as her body weight pushed into them. Lexi gritted her teeth, closed her eyes, and strained even harder, groaning with the effort. Just as she felt she might break free, Das joined the other two boys and forcefully pushed her head down firmly, his fingers digging into her scalp like knives.

"Nooo," she cried, but it was impossible against the three of them, and they soon overpowered her. The wooden top of the stocks was lowered and tightly secured.

Breathing heavily, Lexi slumped forward into the stocks, her head and hands firmly held in place by the rigid structure. Her heart hammered fast in her chest as she took deep breaths in the cooling night air. Trying to turn her head, Lexi found that it was held firmly in place, and she could only look forward or partially to the side. The hole around her neck was too tight to do much more.

As she tried to push away with her legs, she suddenly felt her chin hit the board with a thud, the rough wood pressing into the front of her neck, leaving a red mark. Jakob had childishly kicked her feet out from under her making her fall. Coughing hard, she tried to regain her footing and right her body so she could stand once more.

"That's for scratching me," he sneered. His hot breath was on Lexi's ear as he leaned in close to her. Trying to ignore him, Lexi closed her eyes and swallowed. Her throat was now painfully sore.

Wanting to continue with his taunts, Jakob opened his mouth to say something more; however, Rebekka stepped forward and snapped her fingers at him, directing him to move away. He glared at Lexi once more before quickly stepping back.

Lexi blinked her eyes. It was now completely dark in the square as night had fallen, and the small smattering of stars across the sky gave off very little light. She heard the now familiar sound of a match being struck as Rebekka lit a small kerosene lantern and held it out in front of her.

Rebekka's voice spoke out from the dim light. "As you can see, Lexi, the boys have done a wonderful job setting up a 'punishment' stock here in the town square." Rebekka turned to look at the boys, smiling like a proud parent. "Anyone who refuses to comply will have to spend a few hours here."

Lexi narrowed her eyes. "Comply with what?" She asked incredulously. "What exactly am I *supposed* to have done, Rebekka?"

"You'll make a good example to the others. For some reason, they seem to look up to you." Rebekka lifted a stray piece of hair that had fallen in front of Lexi's face making Lexi flinch. Rebekka laughed.

"Plus, you tried to help a troublemaker," continued Rebekka as she nudged Zac's prone body with her foot. Das, who was watching, dropped his eyes to the ground.

As Lexi listened to Rebekka ranting, she shook the wooden stocks from side to side, trying to break free.

"If you keep doing that, Lexi, we will tie your legs together, and you can stay in there all night," threatened Rebekka, placing her hand on Lexi's head, pushing it down forcefully.

"Get your hand off me," snarled Lexi through gritted teeth. Her hands in tight fists hanging in front of the contraption were now starting to shake.

Rebekka laughed again but removed her hand. "I don't think Lexi is very pleased, boys," she crowed. "Maybe she'll think twice before going against me next time."

"I wasn't going against you; I was just helping a friend."

Just then, Zac sat up groggily. He coughed, spluttered, and rubbed his throat, red and irritated from his hours in the stocks. Looking about in confusion, he soon spotted Lexi and tried to stand. His body swayed unsteadily as he staggered to his feet, his arms outstretched, looking as though he were about to fall.

Lexi tried to turn her head to look at him but could only see his feet with her limited range of vision. "Run, Zac!" she cried out, trying to warn him. "Run!"

Zac looked from Lexi to Rebekka to the boys. He stood swaying like a toddler learning to walk.

As Zac hesitated, Rebekka pointed to Aiden and Jakob. "You two grab him and bring him back to my house," she commanded. "And you stay here and guard *her*," she flicked her hand backwards toward Das, who was standing with his hands in his pockets, shuffling his feet from side to side.

Not waiting to see if Das did as she asked, Rebekka stomped towards Aiden and Jakob, who now had Zac gripped between them. "Come on," she said, leading the way as the two boys dragged Zac behind her. "Hurry up!"

"Wait!" called Lexi. "I can't stay in here; I need my bush brew."

"Not my problem!" replied Rebekka without looking back.

Watching the three of them leave, Das moved over towards Lexi. He reached forward and unbuckled the metal flask attached to her belt.

"Das," whispered Lexi. "Let me out of here. You know this is not right." Her voice was soft and pleading.

Das shook his head. "I can't. Here, take some of your remedy. It's the best I can do."

"Come on, Das, please," Lexi tried again.

Das looked behind him. "No. I can't." He held the flask to her lips. "Here drink it. I can see your hands are starting to shake."

Lexi flicked her eyes sideways to her fingers. Her hands were indeed shaking uncontrollably. She nodded her head and began to drink from the flask. With her neck stretched forward, it was difficult to swallow, and some of the remedy dribbled down her chin and onto the ground sploshing at her feet. She hated wasting the special brew, but in her position, it was the best she could do.

Letting the lukewarm mixture flow down her throat and into her belly, Lexi closed her eyes and waited for the sweet relief the remedy would bring. She breathed in and out in long, slow breaths, trying to will her body to relax. She needed to stay calm and think.

Das watched her closely as she closed her eyes. He folded his arms across his chest, his own hands shaking a little. "That's better, I don't want you going all *crazy* on me."

Lexi's eyes flicked open.

"That's it, Das. You could say I went all crazy and broke free," she clenched her fists once more.

"No way," he said firmly. "I don't want to end up in that thing." He pointed to the stocks.

"Come on, Das. Please let me out," Lexi tried once more.

But Das turned his back on her and crossed his arms, refusing to look at her. Lexi's head dropped forward with fatigue, but she smiled as she stood trapped in the wooden frame. *At least she had managed to free Zac from the contraption.*

Unknown to the two in the square, someone else was watching from the shadows. A young woman with short blonde, cropped hair. Jessica. She wasn't wearing one of the white T-shirts with a red star and didn't ever want to be part of that gang. She preferred to remain hidden in the shadows, biding her time and simply watching and waiting. As soon as the young woman was sure Das wouldn't see her, Jessica slowly stood, turned to face the town, and raced to find Hadley.

Back at the bush camp, Braydon was waiting for Lexi to return. He tapped his hand on his thigh as he peered at the darkening sky, a deep frown crossing his brow. Pushing himself up from the fallen log by the firepit, he started to pace back and forth. At every little noise, his head would jerk around, hoping to see Lexi walking into their campsite with news of what was happening in town.

As the orange glow of sunset bloomed across the sky, Braydon's eyes flicked towards the makeshift path leading into town. "Stuff it," he exclaimed, swatting a mosquito buzzing around his ear. "I can't just sit here and wait any longer."

Pushing himself up from his sitting position and striding purposefully to his tent, Braydon lifted the tent flap, crawled inside, and began shuffling through a bag of goods hanging from the roof tent pole. He pulled out a small towel, a used bar of soap and a comb before finding what he was looking for. A small battery-operated torch. Flicking the switch, Braydon turned it on to check that it was working. The batteries were old, and the torch gave off a muted, yellow glow.

"Well, you'll have to do," he murmured, switching off the light and shrugging.

Clutching the torch in his hand and a full flask of bush remedy, which he had attached to his belt, Braydon strode down the rocky path.

Not long after, he broke through the bushland and onto the wide-open road, his thick curls bouncing on his head as he walked. Soon, he reached the outskirts of town and stopped for a moment. Scratching his chin, Braydon craned his head to the side. He squinted into the darkness, shining his torch down the road. *Had he heard something?*

He breathed in sharply as the muted light showed the dim outline of a figure running towards him from the direction of town. His shoulders clenched.

"Who's there?" he called.

No answer.

"Hey, who is that?!" His voice broke as he hollered.

The other person didn't answer but waved a torch above their head in response as they kept running straight towards him.

Braydon stared out into the gloomy blackness, trying to see more clearly. He hesitated before raising his own torch above his head and waving back.

As the person drew closer, Braydon could see that it was Hadley. His shoulders relaxed and he laughed. "What are you doing out here running around in the darkness?"

Hadley shone her torch into his face. "Oh, thank God," she said in relief. "I thought I was going to have to run all the way to your campsite."

Braydon grimaced in the light and held his hand up to shield his eyes.

"Sorry," said Hadley, dipping her torch light which immediately flickered and dimmed. She groaned and held the torch out in front of her shaking it. "This damn torch keeps going out, and I've been pooping my pants that a dingo was going to leap out of the bushes at me." She put her hands on her knees to catch her breath.

Braydon looked at his own weak torchlight. "Yeah, I don't think this one is going to last for very long either. By the way, have you seen Lexi?"

Hadley nodded her head vigorously, still trying to catch her breath. "I need you to come with me." She grabbed Braydon's hand and started to pull him along the road. "Come on, we have to hurry."

"Wait!" Braydon said, pulling back. "What's going on? Where's Lexi? Has this got something to do with her?"

Hadley stopped pulling and turned to face Braydon, her face confused. "Wait, I thought you knew."

"Knew what?"

"I thought that's why you were coming into town."

Braydon's eyes narrowed. "No. I haven't seen Lexi for a few hours. I've been stuck out in the bush; I don't know anything. Tell me what's going on."

Hadley's eyes flicked to the flask of remedy sitting on Braydon's hip.

"Err, you might want to take a swig of that first," she suggested, her voice wobbling. Hadley dropped his hand and pointed to the flask.

Braydon looked down at the flask where she was pointing and then at the young girl standing in front of him. He took a deep breath. "Hadley," he said calmly. "Tell me what's going on?"

Hadley was now stepping from one foot to the other. She didn't look in the least bit calm. "It's not good." She once again glanced at the flask. "Aiden, Das and Jakob have put Lexi in this punishment thing."

"Punishment thing?" queried Braydon frowning, his hand tightening on his torch.

"In the town square. Come on, I'll show you. We're wasting time standing here." Hadley looked at Braydon pleadingly. "We have to go and help her!"

"What the fuck!" yelled Braydon, his nostrils flaring. "She'd better not be hurt," he said through gritted teeth as he started to sprint down the road with Hadley trying to keep up.

As Braydon's torchlight flitted weakly back and forth across the road as they ran, the two of them finally reached the edge of the town square. Holding up his hand for Hadley to stop, Braydon crouched down, switched off his torch and peered towards the dimly lit scene in the centre of the town square. It looked as though three figures were standing around another figure who was bent forward.

"Is that Lexi?"

Hadley nodded. "Yep, they have her in some sort of wooden restraining thing," she whispered.

Even in the darkness, Hadley could feel the anger and tension radiating from Braydon. She gently touched his arm and said, "Keep your cool, Braydon. We need to be clear-headed to help Lexi."

Braydon didn't look at Hadley but nodded and slowly started to edge closer to the group. He kept his body low and crouched. Hadley's grip on his lower arm tightened as he began to move away.

"Wait," she hissed, grabbing his torch from his hand.

Braydon swivelled to look at her, and Hadley leaned in closer, squatting on her haunches. "We need help. I'm going to go and find Rebekka," she kept her voice low. "I'm sure she doesn't know anything about this," she said, nodding towards the group. "She can help with the boys. I won't be long."

"Wait, Hadley," Braydon reached for Hadley's arm, but she had already stood and scampered away, taking his torch with her. He placed his hands on the ground in front of him and watched her go, his lips drawn together, unsure whether to go after her.

The harsh sound of a boy's laughter drew his attention back to what was happening in the square. With one last look towards Hadley, he let her go and resumed his slow creep forward using the darkness as a shield.

Edging forward bit by bit, trying not to make a sound, Braydon tried to calm his rapid breathing. The closer he got, the more he could see and the angrier he became, his breathing escalating. Around him, the darkness was dense, as though he were in an underground mine. But in the centre of the square, the boys had positioned several glass jars containing long, white, lit candles around the wooden structure, creating a muted, eery glow like the set of a horror movie.

The figure in the stocks stood uncomfortably bent forward with their head low and their long hair hanging loosely in front of them. Even though he couldn't see her face, Braydon was now certain it was Lexi trapped like an animal in that contraption. His hands automatically clenched into tight fists, his jaw hardening. He couldn't wait any longer.

Thrusting himself forward, Braydon quickly stood and strode in big, forceful steps straight towards Lexi and the boys guarding her.

"Hello, Braydon," smirked Das as if expecting him. A sly grin spread across his face. "What brings you here this time of night. You should be in bed."

"What do you think you are doing!" Braydon pointed at Lexi. "Let her out now!" his voice was low, hard, and uncompromising.

"Sure," said Jakob raising his hand to his head in a salute. "Anything you say. SIR."

Braydon ignored him and moved closer to Lexi; his eyes focused only on her. He didn't get very far before someone's hands grabbed him from behind and pinned his arms to his chest. Jakob and Das rushed forward to help and soon wrestled Braydon to the ground, his face slamming into the dirt with a thud. Debris pushed into his cheeks and mouth.

Braydon uttered an ear-splitting yell as he struggled with the three boys pinning him to the ground. "Get off me, you jerk!" he thundered, yanking one of his arms free and hitting Das on the jaw. The boy fell to the side but soon recovered and resumed forcing Braydon's face onto the ground.

"Tie him up!" snarled Jakob, who had his knee planted firmly in the middle of Braydon's back. "There's a rope over there," he said, gesturing to a pile of unused rope not too far away.

"I'll get it," replied Das, rubbing his jaw. "Let's tie him up to the flagpole."

Jakob and Aiden nodded vigorously. "Good idea. Better make sure the knots are tight," they said, dragging Braydon along the ground.

Meanwhile, unaware of Braydon's predicament, Hadley had reached Rebekka's house.

Looking about her, she could see the street was dark and quiet. No one seemed to be about. Hadley swallowed. *Everything felt so different in the darkness.* The children hadn't had electricity in the town for a long time, but the depth of darkness without street and house lights always amazed Hadley. She could barely see in front of her, as Braydon's torchlight had died a few minutes after she had left him. She shook her own torch, trying to will it to life; however, it too had died and wouldn't even give off a faint glow. She glowered at the useless thing before dropping it into the dirt.

Before moving on, Hadley glanced back over her shoulder towards the direction of the town square. She tilted her head to the side and listened but could not hear anything. She hoped Braydon and Lexi were alright.

Turning back to face Rebekka's house again, Hadley moved slowly forward, trying not to trip over anything in the darkness. Carefully placing one foot in front of the other, Hadley tried to feel for fallen branches and potholes in the ground. A sudden burst of noise from an orchestra of nearby crickets made her jump in alarm, and she giggled, placing her hand on her heart. Hadley shook her head. "Come on, you idiot," she muttered to herself. "What are you scared of? The boogieman!" Giggling again, she walked towards the house.

Looking up, all she could see was blackness. The windows were dark, and there wasn't any noise from inside, though everything was now usually much quieter without radios and televisions. Hadley had no idea what time it was as she no longer wore a watch, and mobile phones were only a fond memory.

"I wonder if she's asleep," she murmured, trying to peer through one of the windows. "She'll throw a fit if I wake her." Hadley stood biting her lip. "Maybe I should try and see if she's asleep first."

Stepping back to look at the house once more, Hadley thought she could see a dim glow coming from one side of the house, so she set off to investigate.

Moving slowly, trying not to walk into any bushes or trip over anything lying on the ground, she edged her way around the side of the house. Looking up, Hadley could see a faint flickering light coming from a small side window. This window was smaller and higher up than the other house windows, and she wondered if it was a bathroom one.

Standing on her tiptoes and stretching her arms up, Hadley could just reach the bottom ledge of the windowsill with her fingers, but she was too short to see through.

"Hmph." She dropped her arms by her sides and leaned against the house. She peered out into the darkness before taking a tentative step forward. She needed to find something she could stand on.

Slowly moving around in the darkness with her body bent forward, and her hands stretched out in front of her, Hadley felt around for anything suitable.

Bushes scratched her hands, and low-hanging branches threatened to poke her eyes before her shin painfully connected with something hard. Her hand shot to her mouth, trying to stifle a yelp. Peering down, she could make out a rectangular shape by her feet.

Maybe it was a box.

Bending over, she could see that it *was* indeed a box. An old wooden crate lying on its side in the dirt, and a smile spread across her face.

"Perfect."

Hoping there weren't any spiders inside, she placed her hands on either side of the wooden crate and began dragging it closer to the house. Pushing the box to where she wanted it, Hadley laid it on its side just under the position of the window. Then, carefully placing one foot on the box and a hand on the wall, Hadley slowly stood, testing its sturdiness. The box held. She smiled.

Feeling satisfied, Hadley stood on the box with both feet placing her hands on the wall for balance. Stretching up on her tippy toes, Hadley could just peer into the lit room. It was a bathroom. Four lit candles were sitting on the bathroom cabinet, their orange flames burning brightly; however, no one was in the small room. *Had Rebekka gone to bed and forgotten to blow them out?*

Hadley shrugged. She began to step from the box when she saw someone enter the room. It was Rebekka. She was wearing grey sweatpants, and a navy t-shirt, her feet bare. Instinctively Hadley ducked down. Her fingers gripped the wooden window ledge for balance, and she waited.

After what seemed forever to Hadley, her legs began to ache, so she slowly stood straight again and raised her head, keeping her eyes just above the windowsill. She peered into the room again, her cheeks flaming red as she watched Rebekka's night-time activities.

"What's she doing," murmured Hadley as she spied the woman reaching a hand into her bra and pulling out a transparent glass bottle containing a small amount of brown liquid. Stretching her body further upward, Hadley tried to get a better view. The box wobbled precariously beneath her.

"What *is* that?"

Shaking the vial vigorously, Rebekka unscrewed the cap to reveal a little eyedropper attached to the lid. She squeezed the top of the eyedropper, capturing some of the brown liquid, then brought it close to her right eye. She placed a single drop in one eye and then the other.

Hadley watched transfixed.

Rebekka replaced the lid before tilting her head back and closing her eyes. She breathed in and out deeply.

"Is that for the virus? Is she sick? Why didn't she tell us?"

Hadley continued to watch, rubbing at her own eyes as thoughts and confusion ran through her mind.

Distracted, Hadley forgot where she was and took a step backward. Her right foot slipped on the back edge of the wooden box, and she suddenly felt herself falling! Flailing her arms about her like a windmill, Hadley tried to steady herself, but it didn't help. The air rushed past in a whoosh as gravity took over, and she hit the ground with a hard thump. The wooden crate flew from under her feet, smashing into the wall and cracking loudly.

Laying on her back with the air knocked out of her, Hadley lay stunned, staring up at the little window, her eyes wide. *Did Rebekka hear that?*

Pushing herself up with her hands, Hadley began to sit when a high-pitched squeaking noise made her freeze. Someone had just opened the front door of the house. Hadley quickly lay flat and still.

"Is anyone there?" called Rebekka. "Hello!"

Blinking rapidly, Hadley turned her head towards the voice. "Don't come out here," she whispered before thrusting her hand over her mouth. She held her breath, listening for footsteps. If Rebekka spotted her, she would know she had been spying. Hadley remained frozen on the ground, not daring to move, hoping the bushes near her would shield her body.

"Hello!?" called Rebekka once more. Her voice sounded nearer, her feet crunching on the fallen leaves and debris as she walked. Each step sounded loud in the quietness of the night, and Hadley held her breath.

Rebekka peered out in the darkness in front of her house, listening. She held a small lantern before her; however, it did not give off much light.

As Hadley lay deathly still, staring out into the darkness towards Rebekka, she could feel a tickling sensation crawling over her outstretched hand as if little insect legs were creeping over her skin. Her breath caught in her throat, and her eyes flicked towards her hand. She couldn't see anything in the darkness, but she could feel something! Hadley bit her lip, resisting the urge to flick her hand. Rebekka was now at the corner of the house, not far from where Hadley lay. She had to remain still and quiet.

Swallowing, Hadley tried not to think of the little legs running over her skin. In the corner of her vision, she could see

Rebekka's outline; however, without turning her head, she could not tell if Rebekka was looking at her. Hadley began to sweat.

Rebekka swivelled her head this way and that as she peered into the darkness. She held the lantern up before her trying to see in the blackness of the gathering night. A slight breeze rustled the leaves in the bushes next to her, and she quickly turned to face it, bending over to peer into the foliage. She took a step closer to the bush, and something bit her bare foot. She cursed, slapping at her skin with her hand. Groaning, she took one last look around her before heading back to the front steps of her house and stomping back inside. She slammed the door behind her locking it.

Hadley lay as still as she could until she heard the front door firmly slamming shut. Then, jumping to her feet, she flicked her hand, frantically brushing away the black bull ants with her other hand.

"Thank you for not biting me," she whispered appreciatively before scampering away from the house, her heart thumping, and her head spinning.

What had just happened? What was going on with Rebekka?

"Why was she keeping the eyedrops in her bra?" She murmured, shaking her head. She glanced back at Rebekka's dark house, stepping from one foot to the other. Twisting her hands together, she stared at the house. *Should she go back to Lexi and Braydon? Should she try again with Rebekka, or should she find someone else to help?*

Hadley took a few steps towards the town square before stopping and turning towards Todd's house. She began trotting towards his home, trying to keep to the middle of the road so as not to trip on anything. With the three guys on guard around Lexi, even with Braydon, she was going to need some extra help.

CHAPTER EIGHT

With the sun setting in Jasper's Bay, the evening was finally becoming a little cooler and more bearable. Hadley quickly made her way to Todds house, dodging discarded bicycles and skateboards left by children on the road and paths outside their homes. Without the worry of cars or other vehicles crushing them, the children simply left them scattered about outside.

When Hadley reached Todd's house, she found him asleep in one of the big chairs on his porch. With his head back, and his mouth open he lay gently snoring. Walking up the porch steps, Hadley stifled a laugh. She wished she had a phone to take a photo of him. As she moved closer to him, she touched his arm and called out his name making him startle awake. He jumped to his feet in alarm, knocking a pile of books from the small table by his side.

"What's going on!?" Todd sat back down with a flump. "Oh, Hadley. It's you."

"Yes, it's me. Who did you think it was?"

Wiping a finger across his top lip, he looked at Hadley. "I don't know. I was having a weird dream." He took her hand in his. "What's up. Are you okay? You look worried."

"I am. I need your help. Lexi is in trouble." Hadley proceeded to tell Todd about the three boys holding Lexi captive in the town square and the erection of the "stocks."

Todd rubbed at his chin; his face was thoughtful. "We had better get some of the other boys to help." He stood and hitched up his shorts. "How about Logan and Jason, they live the closest."

Hadley nodded. "Yep, good idea, but we had better hurry," she began to pull Todd down the porch steps. "Braydon is there on his own."

"Right," stated Todd in alarm. "Let's go." He took off running towards the boy's house with Hadley hot on his heels.

Sitting in Logan and Jason's front room, Hadley explained what was going on in the town square, and the boys immediately agreed to help. Jason decided to bring the little dog Polo, and the rescue group set about making their way through the streets in the darkness towards the square.

When they finally arrived, they were surprised to see a large crowd already gathered. Even though it was the middle of the night, and nobody had telephones anymore, news had travelled fast.

"Where's Braydon and Lexi?" asked Hadley, immediately looking around her. She frowned. With so many bodies blocking her view, it was difficult to see anything clearly in the darkness.

"Oh," she said in surprise, blinking a few times. "Rebekka is here, I thought she was still at home. I'll go and ask her for help."

The older woman was standing and talking with a group of children. She was waving her hands around animatedly as if telling a dramatic story. The youngsters in front of her were gazing up at her in awe.

"Weren't you just at her house?" asked Todd.

'Yeah," replied Hadley nodding her head. "But I didn't actually talk to her." Hadley hadn't yet told the others what she had seen at Rebekka's house. She was uncertain precisely what it *was* she had witnessed. She walked towards Rebekka without waiting for the other's response.

Todd watched Hadley walk away. He shrugged and turned back to the others. "Let's have a look around." The group nodded in agreement trying not to get bustled by the growing crowd of onlookers. "Geeze, is every kid in Jasper's Bay here?"

The crowd of children pushed and shoved at each other as they each tried to get a better view as if they were at a rock concert waiting for the main act to arrive.

"What is it with these kids?" Jason remarked as he pushed through the densely packed group. He shoved a boy with a yellow t-shirt out of the way when he refused to let him pass.

"What the…." his eyes widened as they reached the outer edge of the crowd. "Tell me that's NOT Braydon tied up to that flagpole!" He stood for a moment staring at the sight in front of him. "Come on, Logan. You and me, let's go help Braydon. Todd, you go and get Hadley. Try not to draw any attention to yourselves."

Jason didn't wait to see if the others were doing what he asked; he started walking towards the flagpole in big, angry strides. He could see that Braydon had his feet tied in front of him, his hands tied behind his back, and a cloth tied around his mouth to gag him. He had obviously had a lot to say.

Even from a distance, Jason could see that Braydon was fuming just like a pressure cooker with the lid on too tight, about to explode. Logan glanced at Jason as they walked. "Bloody hell, this could get messy."

Jason nodded but kept walking towards their friend.

Just before Jason reached Braydon, Aiden stepped in front of him blocking his way. His arms were folded tightly across his chest, his face scowling.

"Get out of the way, Aiden," demanded Jason, glaring at the younger boy. "We don't tie people up like animals."

"Yeah, well, he shouldn't have acted like one then, should he," responded Matthew coming to stand beside Aiden. He flicked his blonde fringe out of his eyes.

"Look, we don't want any trouble; we just want to make sure Braydon's okay." Logan stood beside Jason and pointed towards Braydon, tied to the post.

"Oh, he's all right," smirked Aiden motioning over his shoulder with his thumb.

Logan shook his head and pushed past Aiden. "Yeah, well, he won't be if he doesn't get some of the bush remedy, will he!"

Braydon had a metal flask of the remedy still strapped to his belt.

"Hey!" exclaimed Aiden in a huff as both boys pushed past him with their shoulders. Jason walked straight up to Braydon, who was breathing heavily and undid the flask from his belt. Braydon flinched as Jason touched him.

"It's alright, mate," whispered Jason. "We've come to help you."

Matthew and Aiden glared at the boys but did not try to stop them. Instead, they watched them momentarily before returning to face the crowd. A commotion on the other side of the square had drawn their attention away. Bending their heads together, they began talking animatedly.

Aiden started to move away. "Don't you dare let him down, Jason," he ordered as he and Matthew trotted away towards the commotion. "We will be back," he called out over his shoulder.

"No worries. We just want to give him some remedy."

Aiden flicked his hand at them dismissively before walking away.

"Here, Braydon," said Jason, pulling the gag from Braydon's mouth and bringing the flask to his lips. Braydon's face was covered in sweat, and his legs were shaking.

Gulping down mouthfuls of the liquid, he looked as though he wanted to start yelling. Jason tried to stop him and quickly brought his finger to Braydon's mouth to quieten him.

"Keep cool, mate," he whispered urgently, glancing behind him. "We are going to get you out of here in a minute, but you've got to be quiet." He nodded his head towards the two boys trotting away. "We don't want *them,* to see."

Braydon looked from Jason to Logan, his wild eyes slowly starting to focus as the remedy took effect. "Okay," he breathed heavily. "Is Lexi alright?" He craned his neck, trying to see through the gathered crowd.

Logan placed his hand on Braydon's arm. "We haven't seen her yet, mate. Hadley and Todd are helping her now."

Braydon's shoulders relaxed, and he nodded. "Okay."

"Right, let's get you out of here," whispered Logan slipping behind Braydon. He started loosening the tight ropes tying Braydon's hands to the flagpole. Jason did his best to block the view with his body. While the dim light and number of children milling around helped shield them, they would be discovered if anyone came too close. Logan tried to work quickly, but the rope was unforgiving, and the knots were tight. It was going to take some time.

Meanwhile, on the other side of the square, Hadley and Todd made their way towards Rebekka, who was smiling and laughing with a group of children gathered around her like flies on a lolly. Hadley noticed several children wearing white Partisan shirts walking around through the crowd of onlookers bumping into them and shoving them as they walked past.

"Rebekka!" she called out as she drew nearer. "We need your help. The boys have put Lexi in those stocks!" she skidded to a stop when she saw the look on Rebekka's face.

Rebekka's lips were pursed together. "Why aren't you wearing your team shirt, Hadley?"

"Oh." Hadley blinked rapidly. "Um, it's dirty, and I haven't washed it," she muttered, looking down at her feet.

"And I suppose yours is dirty too, young man," Rebekka asked, pushing her finger into Todd's chest.

Todd smiled and nodded before taking Hadley's hand in his and squeezing. "I haven't had time to wash it," he said sweetly, his eyes glinting.

"Well, that's not *my* problem. You should be in uniform."

Rebekka looked from Todd's face down to his hand holding Hadley's. Her eyes narrowed as she studied them both. Todd saw the look on Rebekka's face and quickly dropped Hadley's hand, letting his hang loosely by his side.

Hadley cleared her throat, trying to be heard amongst the commotion of children around them. "Er, Rebekka. Lexi is…"

"I *know* where she is," interrupted Rebekka. "She's where she belongs."

Hadley's mouth dropped open, and she stared at the older woman's face in confusion. Rebekka's eyes looked cold and hard, and her face held no emotion.

Hadley swallowed. "You knew!"

"Hadley, I put her there. Now, run along, will you," Rebekka turned her back. "I'm done talking," she flicked her hand in the air as if she were royalty.

Staring hard at Rebekka's back for a few moments, Hadley's cheeks flushed. She turned towards Todd. "Come on," she whispered, nudging him. "Let's go and help Lexi ourselves."

Looking around the crowd of faces, Hadley saw Jessica approaching her. Jessica had come to Hadley's house earlier in the evening and informed her what the boys were doing to Lexi, and she trusted her to be honest.

Jessica held out her hand as she pushed through the throng of children. "Hadley," she breathed heavily. "I've been looking for you. Lexi is straight through there." She grabbed Hadley's arm and twisted her around until she faced the correct way. She pointed with an outstretched hand. "Be careful. Das and Jakob are guarding her." Jessica shook her head. "You'd better hurry, Hadley. She's not in a good way," her mouth turned downwards sadly.

Hadley squeezed Jessica's shoulder, who nodded. "Come on, I'll show you where," she said as she started to push her way back through the crowd.

"Let's go, Todd," Hadley urged as she grabbed his hand. "You're going to have to distract those boys."

Someone stepped on Hadley's toe, and she angrily shoved them away. "Hey, watch it!" she snarled as she wove her way through the onlookers as Jessica made a path through them. The smell of bad breath and sweat filled her nostrils as the children hemmed in on each other, trying to see the spectacle before them.

As Jessica made space through the group, Hadley caught sight of the tall boy Jakob and knew she must be getting closer to Lexi. Her heartbeat quickened, and her palms began to feel sticky. She rubbed them on the back of her shorts.

Jakob stood stiffly with Das positioned beside him as though they were soldiers guarding a prisoner of war instead of one of their own townspeople. Hadley's eyes narrowed. She tried to peer past them; however, their bodies and the crowd were blocking her vision, and all she could see of Lexi was her bent arm and the side of the wooden contraption.

"Hey, losers!" yelled Todd suddenly as he spotted Das and Jakob. He quickly ran towards them. "I thought we were done with this bullying shit."

Das and Jakob quickly swivelled around to face Todd; smirks spread across their faces like deranged clowns. As Hadley saw the boys turn away from Lexi, she took her opportunity. Tiptoeing, she quickly made her way towards her sister.

"What did you call us, Todd?" snapped Das pointing at the other boy. His left hand was curled into a fist by his side.

"I called you a loser, Das. And you too, Jakob!"

Jakob and Das took a few more steps towards Todd. A few more steps away from Lexi.

Hadley could see them move from the corner of her eye. She breathed out a sigh of relief and moved more quickly. Her eyes flicked back towards the stocks. Lexi looked terrible. Her hair had come out of her scrunchie and had fallen around her face in long strands. Her face looked pale and clammy, and her eyes were closed. Even her body looked defeated as it slumped forward in the wooden frame with her hands flopping forward.

Hadley's heart rate quickened. She had to do something fast.

Covering the last few steps in a run, not caring if the boys saw her, she reached into her pocket to retrieve the small silver flask of remedy she had brought with her. She brushed Lexi's loose hair from her face.

"It's all right," she said as Lexi opened her eyes in alarm. "Drink this. It's not much, but it's better than nothing at all." Hadley brought the open flask to Lexi's cracked lips and tilted it so she could drink some of the cool fluid within.

Lexi swallowed deeply, emptying the flask quickly. "Thanks," she grimaced and ran her tongue over her dry lips before dropping her head again.

Hearing a commotion behind them, Hadley glanced over her shoulder to see Todd and the other boys quarrelling. Todd was putting on a good show waving his arms around animatedly and talking loudly.

"Come on, Lexi," she whispered, turning back to her sister. "Let's get you out of this contraption." She tucked Lexi's hair behind her ear.

Lexi peered up into Hadley's face, her eyes were unfocused as if she did not recognise who was speaking to her.

"Lexi, it's me. Hadley." Hadley's eyebrows were pulled together in concern. "You'll be all right, sis. We just need to get you free from this thing and find you some more bush brew."

Working quickly, Hadley ran her eyes over the punishment device holding her sister. Her fingers examined the top and side of the wooden frame until she found what she was looking for, the metal catch. She breathed in sharply, glancing behind her again before quickly sliding the bolt across and lifting the heavy wooden top, releasing Lexi.

Lexi immediately bolted upright, then stepped back, wobbling, and swaying unsteadily on her feet. She rolled her neck, trying to release the tension. Her vertebrae made a loud cracking noise making her wince.

Hadley quickly walked towards Lexi with her arms outstretched. As she stepped forward, her foot kicked something, making a clunking metal noise. She looked down to see what it was. A metal flask spun close to her foot, and Hadley bent to retrieve it. She shook the container, hearing liquid inside. Unscrewing the lid, she brought it to her nose and sniffed. The liquid smelled of berries. It was some of Lexi's bush brew!

"Yes!" grinned Hadley passing the flask to Lexi. "Here, drink this." She offered the half-empty container to Lexi, who nodded, breathing out slowly through her mouth.

Lexi carefully brought the container to her parched lips, not wanting to spill any of the precious liquid. As the cool metal touched her mouth, the sudden sound of harsh laughter nearby drew her attention, and she paused before drinking.

"You know that's a waste of the town's resources," scoffed someone loudly.

Lexi turned to see Rebekka standing with her arms folded across her chest. She was staring at Lexi through slitted eyes. "No one should be made to gather supplies for only a few."

Taking a quick drink, Lexi shook her head slowly. "Rebekka. Everyone is going to need this remedy sooner or later. Eventually, every child here will turn seventeen and succumb to the virus."

Lexi looked directly at Jakob, who was standing closely beside Rebekka. She noticed his knuckles were bloody. "Jakob, you're going to turn seventeen in a few weeks," she reminded him. "You saw what the virus did to Elisha; she went feral. The herbs are the only way we can control it. At least for a short while."

Jakob dropped his eyes to the ground and shuffled his feet from side to side refusing to look at Lexi.

"Sounds like witchcraft to me," taunted Rebekka, looking around at the others. "Do you know what they used to do to witches?" she crowed loudly, a nasty grin on her face.

"Listen, Rebekka," interrupted Lexi before Rebekka could continue and cause more trouble. "Not everyone is immune like you; we *need* this bush medicine."

Rebekka rolled her eyes. "Not my problem."

A crowd of children had now gathered closely from all parts of the town square, pushing and shoving each other as they strained to get a better view. Many were frightened, wide-eyed and unsure as they looked between Lexi and Rebekka. A few of the younger ones held hands and huddled in small groups. Over to the side, Todd stood with his nose bloody and dripping. He leaned forward and pinched the top of his nose with his right finger and thumb as he tried to stench the flow.

Reaching over, Hadley held Lexi's shoulder to steady her. She leaned in close and whispered into Lexi's ear, using her hand to shield their conversation.

As Hadley spoke, Lexi listened intently, her eyes narrowing. She pulled away and looked at Hadley, who nodded. Lexi's lips pursed, her nostrils flaring.

"So, Rebekka," stated Lexi raising her voice and standing with her shoulders back. "Is there anything you'd like to tell us? For instance, are you sick? Maybe you're not immune at all!" Several children in the crowd gasped. The rest fell silent.

"I don't have anything to say to you."

Hadley took a step towards Rebekka. "I saw you, Rebekka."

"What?"

"I saw you with your little eyedropper."

Rebekka sneered. "I knew someone was spying on me!"

Hadley's face turned red. "I wasn't spying. I came to ask you for help."

Hadley's eyes turned angry as Rebekka laughed at her with an ugly sneer spread across her face.

Lexi could see Hadley's anger and quickly stepped between the two women. "So, what exactly are the drops for, Rebekka?" she asked.

Rebekka stood silently for a moment, watching Lexi before replying. "It's medicine. I used to work for a big pharmaceutical company."

Lexi took a small step forward, her eyes brightened. "Is it a cure for the virus?" she held her hand out before her.

"There is no cure."

"A remedy then. Something to delay the effects."

Rebekka only smiled.

"Can you make it?" Lexi's voice rose.

Reaching into her bra with her hand, Rebekka pulled out the small glass bottle. "Guess there's no point in hiding it." She wiggled the bottle in the air. "Last one, I'm afraid. And there's not much left." She smiled again. "It was a prototype. We didn't get the chance to test it and make it before the virus took hold of everyone."

Lexi dropped her hand to her side, her eyes staring at the ground. "You're such a hypocrite," she said as her gaze flicked back to Rebekka. "The way you were bad-mouthing our remedy," she said pointing her finger at the older woman. "You made me feel ashamed for asking the other kids to help collect the herbs."

"Ah, well. Your remedy doesn't work on me, does it."

"How do you know. It might."

"Nope. Already tried it. I took a few of your bottles from your campsite and tried them." Rebekka scratched her nose. "When they didn't work, I poured them down the sink. Useless stuff." She sniffed and shook her head.

Lexi's mouth dropped open. "Do you know how long it takes to make that bush brew? You are such a selfish bitch!"

Rebekka's eyes narrowed, becoming steely hard. "What did you just call me?!"

Lexi stood her ground as she folded her arms across her chest. "You heard me. You're a selfish bitch!"

One of Rebekka's eyes started to twitch. She stood glaring at Lexi for a moment before storming towards her. The dust billowed at her feet as she thundered forward.

Stopping close to Lexi, so close that her breath blew onto her face, Rebekka glared angrily at her. Her top lip curled up into a snarl. Lexi stared right back, refusing to move. No one in the crowd of children said a word. The tension in the air was almost touchable; it was that thick.

Hadley's eyes darted between each woman, and she opened her mouth to say something when all of a sudden, Rebekka took a small step backwards, abruptly raised her right hand in the air and brought it down with a stinging blow across Lexi's face with lightning speed.

One of the children screamed as Lexi's head snapped to the side, several calling out in horror. Lexi staggered sideways before losing her balance and falling to the ground. Her body hit the hard earth with a horrible thump, and her head flung back, hitting the sharp edge of the base of the wooden stocks. The noise her skull made when hitting the corner was ugly.

"Lexi!" Hadley's eyes grew wide as she watched her sister fall. She turned her gaze on Rebekka, whose hand had turned into a tight fist as she stood motionless, staring at the fallen Lexi.

"What have you done!" yelled Hadley, running to Lexi's side. "Rebekka. What have you done!"

CHAPTER NINE

"Lexi!" yelled Hadley, dropping to her knees beside the fallen girl. She placed her hands upon her shoulders and frantically shook them. "Open your eyes!"

A hush had fallen over the children of Jasper's Bay as they silently milled around, trying to see what was happening. As the children jostled each other for a better position, one of the boys lost his footing and fell like a chopped tree onto Lexi's outstretched legs as she lay on her back. Lexi moaned. "Hadley?" her voice was quiet and shaky.

"Get off her!" yelled Hadley through gritted teeth. She stood and roughly pulled the boy away from Lexi's body. "Move back," she said, pointing her finger at his chest, glaring furiously at him.

"OK, you lot," added Todd, whose nose had finally stopped bleeding. He stood beside Hadley and spread his arms wide. "Take a couple of steps back. Lexi needs some room to breathe."

A few of the children did as they were asked, but most stood their ground, continuing to shove each other.

"Hadley?" murmured Lexi again. She slowly opened her eyes and tried to sit up, using her hands to steady herself. "I don't feel so good."

Hadley immediately forgot the boy and dropped back to Lexi's side, her knees hitting the hard ground with a thud. She placed her arms around Lexi's shoulders and helped her sit. "Here, let me help you. Just take it slow. You've had a bad knock."

"I'm really dizzy."

"Yeah, well, you hit your head pretty hard." Hadley tucked Lexi's wayward hair behind her ear.

Just then, a loud commotion to their side made both girls turn their heads.

"What's going on?" stammered Braydon as he pushed through the crowd. Jason and Logan were close behind him having managed to free him from the flagpole. He took one look at Lexi's pale face and rushed to her side, grabbing her hand in his.

"I just feel a bit woozy and have a thumping headache, that's all," she explained, giving him a weak smile. "I'll be all right in a minute. I took a fall like a big clumsy clown."

Braydon's eyes flicked to Hadley.

"She hit her head. Rebekka slapped her. Hard!"

Braydon's nostrils flared, and his cheeks flamed a ruddy red colour. "Let me see, Lexi," he said, tilting her forward so he could examine the back of her head. The darkness of the night made it difficult to see anything clearly, so he placed his fingers on the back of her skull and carefully felt around.

"Ouch!" Lexi winced, her face screwing up. She breathed in sharply.

"Sorry, Lexi," said Braydon, his voice gentle. He removed his hand and looked down. He could feel a stickiness between his fingers. Bringing his hand closer to his eyes, he saw his fingers were covered in oozy blood. Lexi's blood.

Staring at his fingers, Braydon slowly closed them into a tight fist. He stood abruptly and turned to find Rebekka. His eyes scanned the crowd for the woman before spotting her surrounded by kids in white shirts. He shook his head. Even after what she had done, they were still protecting her and doing her will. Braydon's fist closed even tighter as he stomped towards her. However, three boys barred his path before he could come close, Jakob, Das, and Aiden. They were the three boys who had tied him to the post earlier.

Braydon's eyes narrowed as he glared at them. "Get out of my way," he said through gritted teeth.

"Oh, no, you don't, Braydon," replied Jakob. "You're going to stay right there." Jakob pointed his finger at the ground in front of Braydon.

Braydon stood stiffly with his clenched fists by his side. "Go to hell, Jakob!" he yelled.

When Braydon began to move closer, the three boys rushed forward and forcefully grabbed his arms. They wrestled him to the ground, ripping his shirt and pinning his thrashing body to the floor.

"Get off me!" yelled Braydon kicking out with his feet.

All around the square, small fights and arguments had broken out between the children of Jasper's Bay as they continued to push and shove at each other. Some of the younger children had started to cry and ran to the outer edges of the square away from the fighting.

"Hadley!" cried Lexi, grabbing her sister's arm with her hand, her voice shook. "There's blood coming from my ear!" Her fingers touched her ear gingerly as a trickle of blood seeped from within. Lexi's eyes widened as she looked at Hadley in alarm.

"I don't know what that means," moaned Hadley, her face full of concern. She twisted Lexi's head to the side to look at the oozing blood.

"She's probably got swelling on the brain," Rebekka spoke firmly as she moved closer to the girls. She had left the fighting boys to stand near the sisters.

"What?!" asked Hadley, turning her head to face her.

"Hitting your head that hard might cause swelling." She shrugged, looking bored.

Hadley stared at her. "How can you be so calm and unfeeling?"

Rebekka shrugged again, her face blank.

"You *are* a bitch!"

A small moan escaped Lexi's lips, and she once again grabbed Hadley's arm as she leaned back against the wooden structure of the stocks. Her shoulders sagged, and her body slumped like a deflated balloon.

"Lexi?" Hadley stammered, lifting her drooping head. She brushed her hair out of her eyes. "You have to stay awake."

Lexi's eyes started closing as though she were struggling to keep them open.

"Come on, Lexi. Stay awake!" Hadley shook her sister's shoulder roughly. "We need you. *I* need you!" Her bottom lip started to wobble.

As Hadley continued talking, Lexi's eyes fluttered open. The sun had finally started to rise in the east, giving beautiful pink and orange hues on the horizon as a new morning broke. Her eyes flicked from Hadley's face to the gorgeous pastel pinks of the sky. The early morning clouds looked like an artist's painting, making her smile. She breathed a settling breath as she reached up to touch Hadley's cheek.

Lexi's face had become very pale. "You're going to be all right, Hadley. You've always been strong; you just need to remember that."

Hadley shook her head. "No, I'm not," she whispered as tears formed in her eyes. "I don't want to be alone, don't leave me, Lexi."

Jason and Logan came to squat by Hadley and Lexi's side. Jason looked between his two friends. He had tears in the corner of his eyes as he placed one hand on Lexi's thigh and the other on Hadley's shoulder and squeezed. "You won't be alone, Hadley. You have us."

Lexi rested her hand on Jason's. He looked towards her, and she nodded slightly. "I'm sure glad we picked you up hitchhiking from the side of the road last year," she said, her voice almost a whisper and she smiled once more, her eyes slowly closing.

"I'm glad you did, too," agreed Jason, tears now streaming down his face. He wiped his nose with the back of his hand. "Look who is here, Lexi," Jason said urgently as he held up their little dog Polo.

Lexi's eyes opened a little, and Jason held the wiggling dog close to her face so she could see him clearly. She smiled as Polo licked her cheek with his pink, raspy tongue. His tail swished back and forth, hitting Jason's arm.

As Polo grew heavy in his outstretched arms, Jason placed him on the ground by Lexi's side.

"You troublemaker," she whispered, reaching out for him but missing. Her hand falling to her side.

Hadley leaned over and gently placed Lexi's hand on Polo's head.

Feeling the soft fur between her fingers, Lexi stroked the little dog's head, playing with his ears. Polo whined softly and rested his head on her leg before looking up at her with his gentle brown eyes.

In the background, Hadley could hear Braydon and the other boys continuing to fight. It sounded like a war was going on with all the yelling and cursing, and she leaned in closer to Lexi so she could hear her.

Hadley took a deep breath. "You know, Lexi," she said, biting her lower lip. "I wasn't *really* with Rebekka and the Partisans at all. I was always with you. I joined them for fun, but I preferred to be spying on them."

Hadley took Lexi's hand in hers. It felt weirdly cold. "Just like that TV show, we used to watch when we were kids. Remember? It was called Totally Spies. Mum and Dad were always telling us to turn the volume down because we kept singing the theme song so loudly." Hadley started to laugh as she leaned back to look at Lexi's face to see if she was laughing too. "Do you remember?"

But Lexi hadn't heard. Her face had turned ashen, her head had fallen to the side and her eyes were closed for the last time.

Dropping her face into her hands, Hadley sank back onto the ground. She felt as though someone had just punched her in the stomach. *How could someone so young and full of life die so easily?*

She let her hands fall to her sides and stared at the sky. Fat tears ran unchecked down her cheeks as a heartfelt moan escaped her lips.

At that moment, Braydon managed to break away from Jakob and Das and shoved his way through the crowd of onlookers. He saw Rebekka standing as still as a stone statue staring off into space, he saw the backs of Jason and Logan sitting on the ground, and he saw Hadley. One look at her face told him Lexi was gone. He rushed to her and dropped down by her side, the skin scrapping from his knees as he sank to the ground. Quickly reaching forward, he pulled Lexi into his arms.

"No, Lexi. No!" he moaned, burying his face in her hair. "I didn't get to say goodbye." Pulling Lexi tighter, Braydon let out an anguished yell.

CHAPTER TEN

As Hadley and Braydon cradled Lexi's body between them. Logan and Jason stood to look for Rebekka, only to find she was nowhere in sight, and neither was Jakob. Almost all the other kids in the Partisan group were milling around the square, like lost souls looking at each other for guidance.

All the other town children had formed a tight circle around Lexi, Braydon, and Hadley, facing outwards. They glared at the kids in white shirts with red stars. Their displeasure was apparent on their faces. The town of Jasper's Bay remained divided.

Several Partisans, including Das, slowly began to pull the white shirts from their bodies and drop them on the ground. They folded their arms around their chests and looked about sheepishly.

Das walked forward towards the circle surrounding Lexi.

"I'm sorry, Hadley," he said, sounding genuinely remorseful as he pushed through the circle and walked towards her.

"Don't you come near me, Das," threatened Hadley, her face blotchy. "You helped put Lexi in that contraption." She pointed at the wooden stocks standing empty behind her.

Das swallowed. He hung his head and looked at the ground. "I know, and I can't change that, but I can help now."

Some children from the circle had moved towards the stocks and begun to push and pull at the immovable wooden structure. Das walked towards them, squatted, and began to use his hands to dig at the soil holding the legs of the frame. The others looked at him suspiciously before bending over to help him.

Braydon, his face, hands and even his shoes splattered with blood, grunted but refused to look away from Lexi. He held her tightly in his arms as he fought back tears that threatened to spill forth like a broken dam at any moment. He stared at Lexi's lifeless face in disbelief at what had just happened, his eyes glassy and unfocused.

Hadley, with her eyes full of tears, refused to release Lexi's hand as she crouched beside Braydon and her sister. Her knuckles were turning white as she clung fiercely to Lexi, hoping she would sit up at any moment and yell at Rebekka, Jakob, and Das.

Getting to his feet, Jason leaned forward and put his hand tenderly on Hadley's shoulder. "Hadley," he said in a wobbly voice. "The sun has risen now." He looked towards the eastern horizon as the pinks and oranges faded into a light, bright blue. "Lexi can't stay out here in the heat."

Hadley turned her head to look at Jason, a frown creasing her brow. She stared at him before slowly nodding her head and sighing.

"Let's bring her to our house," suggested Logan, leaning in to talk quietly to Hadley. "It's the closest." He stood straight and looked at Jason. "We can bury her in the town cemetery later this afternoon."

Hadley let out a mournful noise from deep in her throat.

Having remained silent until now, Braydon slowly stood with Lexi cradled in his arms. "I'll carry her," he said, his voice breaking. His hair was matted to his forehead with sweat, a nasty blue bruise was forming under his left eye, and his top lip was split. He looked terrible.

Jason reached over and placed his hand cautiously on Braydon's forearm. "I've got a few bottles of remedy at the house," he looked into the other boy's glazed, bloodshot eyes. "You should have some."

Braydon didn't reply. He continued to stare at Lexi in confusion.

As he began to move forward, his feet dragging, Hadley, clinging to Lexi's hand, stood still and silent. Her shoulders slumped.

"It's alright, Hadley," Braydon whispered, turning his head towards her. "I won't drop Lexi."

Hadley stared at him, blinking. "I should collect some wildflowers for her," she said quietly. "Pink and White everlastings. They are her favourite."

"I can help you, Hadley," offered Jessica moving to stand by her. She placed her hand over Hadley's. "Let Braydon take Lexi to Jason and Logan's house now."

"Okay," spluttered Hadley sniffing back tears. She shifted her gaze to Jessica but could not let go of her sister's hand.

Braydon shifted his weight to his right leg as Lexi grew heavy in his outstretched arms. He grunted at the effort of holding her.

"Come on, Hadley," soothed Jason, putting his arm around her slumped shoulders. "You can let her go for a little while. Come to our house as soon as you've gathered the flowers." The corners of Jason's eyes were filled with tears, and he wiped them away with the back of his other hand.

Hadley nodded slowly, tears running unchecked like rivers down her red cheeks. She turned towards Braydon, carefully placed Lexi's hand across her still chest, and let go. "I'll see you soon, Sis," she sobbed, wiping her nose with her sleeve.

Turning on her heel, Hadley followed Jessica in the direction of the old schoolyard, where blooms of Everlasting flowers were growing like a stunning carpet of pink and white.

Pushing past the groups of children standing silently watching, Hadley noticed the scattered white partisan shirts lying in the dust. She shook her head.

How had things become so out of control?

Reaching the edge of the group, Hadley pushed past the last few children gathered at the corner of the square and her eyes opened wide in disbelief.

Was that Rebekka carrying a box full of food?

Jakob stood next to her with his arms loaded with another full box!

"Hey!" called out Hadley. "What are you doing with that food?!" Hadley stormed towards the pair, with Jessica following close behind.

The group of children standing nearby turned to look at what was happening. When they saw it was Rebekka, they immediately began to follow Hadley, and soon a larger group formed behind her.

Rebekka, who looked as though she was going to ignore Hadley, slowly turned around to face her and the others. She jutted her chin out in defiance.

"Are you talking to me, Hadley?" she asked snidely.

Hadley glared at her. "Yes, I'm talking to you, Rebekka. Obviously!"

The two women stood scowling at each other like a Western showdown. Rebekka firmly gripping the loaded box, and Hadley with her fists clenched as her arms hung by her sides.

"Rebekka, you're a murderer!" Todd called out from the crowd of children.

"You should be put in those stocks!" yelled another voice.

Rebekka's eyes widened slightly at this, her gaze moving from Hadley to the crowd. She cleared her throat. "I think because of this *thing* with Lexi, I've decided it would be best if I left Jasper's Bay and continued north," she said in a loud, steady voice.

Hadley frowned. "It wasn't just a THING. Your violence caused my sister's death! You could at least say you're sorry!" Hadley's voice trembled, and she crossed her arms across her chest, hugging her body for comfort.

She turned back to look across the town square where Lexi had fallen but Braydon and the other boys had already gone. Her heart started to hammer in her chest, and she felt as though she were about to be sick. Closing her eyes, Hadley swallowed and took a slow, deep breath. She thought about Lexi and remembered what she had said to her before she died. *"You are strong, Hadley. You have always been strong."*

Right now, Hadley didn't feel especially strong but, in some way, she felt as though Lexi were still with her. Two sisters together. As though she were standing by her side right at that moment and it gave her the strength she needed. Hadley's stomach began to slowly unknot. She pulled her hunched shoulders back and stood tall.

Opening her eyes and unfolding her arms, Hadley swivelled back around to face Rebekka and Jakob. She took a couple of steps closer to them and pointed her finger. "You need to leave our town Rebekka. You can go too if you want Jakob, but you're not taking that food with you," her voice was steady. "We have all worked hard for that, it belongs to the kids of Jasper's Bay. Not you!"

Rebekka laughed. "I'll do what I please, Hadley."

Hadley stormed forward with Jessica at her side. Many of the town's kids joined her.

She firmly placed her hands on the box Rebekka was carrying and wrenched it away.

"Oh no, you won't, Rebekka. You have taken enough from us. From *ME*, already!" Hadley turned and placed the box in Jessica's hands, who swiftly moved away, carrying the food out of Rebekka's reach.

Taking Hadley's lead, Todd ran to Jakob and quickly grabbed the box of food. Jakob held on tightly for a brief moment, his knuckles white and straining, before releasing his grip and reluctantly letting the carton go. He didn't say a single word.

"But we will starve," complained Rebekka, her voice not so defiant now.

Hadley stared at her, a small smile playing on her lips. "That's not *my* problem, Rebekka."

Swivelling on her heels, Hadley turned her back and started to walk away. Rebekka narrowed her eyes and glared after her. She looked at the hostile crowd of children before her, no longer happy and welcoming.

Rebekka slowly nodded before turning away from the group. "Come on, time to go," she commanded Jakob as she stalked away from the children without saying another word.

Several kids in the crowd cheered, and a few moved forward to pat Hadley on the back.

"You've changed," remarked one of the children, staring at her.

Hadley stopped walking and turned to face them.

Jessica placed her hand gently on Hadley's arm. "For the better!" she said with a smile.

"Yeah, well," said Hadley, watching a flock of Red-tailed black Cockatoos fly across the blue sky. One of Lexi's favourite birds. She smiled.

"I learned from the best."

THE END

AUTHOR PAGE

Suzanne was born in Perth Western Australia and as a young adult grew up in the small country town of Tom Price situated in the outback of Western Australia.

Suzanne has a Bachelor of Science Degree, and her interests include hiking, photography, and running. She also enjoys going to science fiction conventions!

Suzanne has an adventurous spirit and has had the opportunity to experience many exciting adventures including swimming with Whale Sharks on Ningaloo reef, climbing to Mt Everest base camp in Nepal, descending into one of the pyramids at Giza in Egypt, flying in a hot air balloon over the Valley of the Kings, parachuting from a plane at 12000 feet in York, Western Australia and sitting on the edge of an active volcano on Tanna island in Vanuatu!

In 2018 Suzanne won the award for best Sci fi/Horror in an e-book in the New Apple literary awards for her YA novel

Seventeen and received a bronze medal from Readers' Favorite International Writers' Literary competition for her children's novel *The Pirate Princess and the Golden Locket*.

In 2020, she was a finalist in the International Independent Book Awards and was awarded a Book Excellence Award in Pre-Teen Literature for the *Pirate Princess and the Golden Locket*. Her YA novel *Seventeen* was awarded a Bronze medal in Science Fiction in the Readers' Favorite International Book Awards.

In 2023 Suzanne produced the Australian feature film The Canary.

Suzanne is a member of the Society of Children's Book Writers and Illustrators, the Travel Writers Association, Australian Society of Authors, and the Australian Science Fiction Society.

Her published works include;

Seventeen, book one in the *Seventeen Series*. A YA dystopian adventure story set in Australia.

Rage, book two in the *Seventeen Series*.

Unity, book three in the *Seventeen Series*.

The Pirate Princess and the Golden Locket, a pirate adventure story for middle grade children

The Pirate Princess and the Sirens' Song, the second book in the *Pirate Princess* adventures.

Prepping your family for an emergency. A guide for keeping your home and family safe during a natural disaster, lockdown, or power outage.

Tokyo Travels. A parent's guide for a fun family holiday. Tips and ideas for family travel in Tokyo, Japan.

Suzanne's author website www.Suzanneloweauthor.com

Instagram www.instagram.com/suzannelowe.author/

Facebook www.facebook.com/suzanneloweauthor/

Suzanne Lowe

Seventeen

Book one in the *Seventeen* Series

Winner of the New Apple YA horror/Sci-Fi award

Imagine a world where everything you grew up with is gone. No adults, no internet, no rules. Could you survive?

The world is facing the deadliest virus ever known.

When the KV17 virus kills everyone above the age of seventeen, life becomes a battle of survival for the children left behind. Seeking to escape the escalating violence in the city, two sisters, Lexi and Hadley flee to the Australian outback. Finding sanctuary in the small town of Jasper's Bay, they soon realise it is far from safe, as a gang of lawless teenagers terrorise the town.

Caught in a bitter feud leading to betrayal, deceit and murder, the girls must quickly uncover who their enemies are, and who they can trust. In a world drastically changed from everything they once knew; can the sisters and children of Jasper's Bay learn to adapt? Can they maintain control of their town, and protect it from those who would destroy it?

www.suzanneloweauthor.com

www.silvergumpublishing.com

RAGE

Suzanne Lowe

Rage
Book two in the Seventeen Series

"Let me out of here!" screamed Lexi spit flying from her mouth. Her hair was plastered to her face with sweat, and her face was pink from the heat.

With the KV17 virus now in its mutated form, the lives of Lexi and the older children of Jasper's Bay are under serious threat.

As they fight to find a cure, Lexi is unexpectantly caught up in a cowardly, unprovoked attack. The resulting chain of events leave her shocked and humiliated. Will the rage and fury she feels lead to disastrous consequences, or will her friends rescue her in time?

Is there any hope for those who contract the virus? Lexi thinks so, however, how can they fight an enemy that is invisible?The exciting and compelling YA series set in the harsh Australian outback

The Pirate Princess and The Golden Locket

Book one in the *Pirate Princess* Series.

The first thrilling tale of adventure, friendship, and mystery in the Pirate Princess series.

The Pirate Princess and the Golden Locket is an exciting adventure story for 6-11-year-old children.

Meet Lotty, the brave young orphan whose life is suddenly about to change forever.

When on her twelfth birthday, Lotty is unexpectantly cast out from the Sevenoaks Home for Children, she befriends a cheeky little dog called Mr Jacks. Her life soon becomes an exciting adventure as together they encounter lazy pirates, hidden treasure and uncover the mystery of Lotty's golden locket!

The Pirate Princess and the Golden Locket is a story full of loveable characters, swashbuckling adventures, and ruthless pirates!

https://www.amazon.com/stores/Suzanne-Lowe/author/B01N6O6U52

118

Tokyo Travels

A parent's guide
for a fun family holiday

SUZANNE LOWE

Tokyo Travels

A parent's guide for a fun family holiday.

Talking robots, cartoon characters, ancient temples, and interesting food, Tokyo is an amazing place to visit, but where should you start?Tokyo Travels is a guidebook written for families wanting to travel together. Full of useful tips and practical advice with sections for younger children, teenagers, and young adults.

This guidebook contains:
Packing Tips
Free activities to do with children
Character themed cafes
Best shopping spots
Places to visit in popular areas of Tokyo
How to navigate the train system
Eating out with kids
Health and safety whilst on holiday
and much more!

Tokyo Travels will provide you with practical tips, help you plan your trip, and get you started on your family holiday to Tokyo.

Australian spelling is used throughout